Holding The Horse

J L Williams

Cave Books, an imprint of Ocean Echo Books

A catalogue record of this book is available from the National Library of New Zealand.

ISBN (POD) 978-0-473-62768-3

ISBN (Epub) 978-0-473-62770-6

Praise for Holding The Horse

A gripping story that will have you cheering for Sid all the way. A racing good book for anyone who loves horses, history or characters with grit and determination.
Philippa Werry, award winning author

There is nothing clichéd here. This story is full of emotion. An important story about PSTD, dreams and ambitions, and making do. All this resonates with the modern-day world we are now entering.
Janice Marriott, award winning author and mentor

The history is accurate, the plot and the characters are interwoven to portray the social issues of the time, and the decisions, regrets, and triumphs that Sid goes through reflect real life. The book is a gripping read with good characterisation, action and conflict, and the language is a pleasure to read.
Diana Menefy, award winning author

Set in rural New Zealand in 1946 this story is both engaging and engrossing. Sid's father, not long home from the war, is struggling to cope with a return to a life that now offers few opportunities: his own shadowed past sets him against his son's ambition of becoming a famous jockey. Without know-ing the reasons for his father's opposition, Sid does all he can to realise his dream, even to the extent of putting everything he hopes for in jeopardy. The story's momentum is carried swiftly along by pacy dialogue; persuasive family dynamics, including issues concerning a small deaf sibling; a dash of happy coincidence, as well as a low-key romance between Sid and the daughter of a local horse owner. The historical background of returned soldiers suffering PTSD, as well as feeling generally abandoned by officialdom, is convincing. With a neatly constructed, satisfying plot this exciting story is also a warm-hearted tale that should have wide appeal.

Bill Nagelkerke, award winning children's author, translator and former children's librarian

Dedication

To my father, Bill McLaren
and my uncle, Brian McLaren
for the stories and memories
of a happy childhood.

Contents

Chapter One

Moongazing

"Mum, we're back. The river was freezing!" Sid dumped his towel on the kitchen floor and ran down the hall. "I'm just getting my jumper," he called.

He flung open the bedroom door and froze. The wall with his collection of newspaper cuttings was bare. Only shreds of newsprint now hung from drawing pins. The faded green and gold wallpaper was peppered with dark patches where his precious cuttings had been pinned. He stared around wildly, then hurtled back to the kitchen.

"Who did it?"

"Sid, dear..." Mum smoothed her hair back from her forehead. "Your father..."

"He did that?"

His mother spread her hands. "I tried to tell him they were important to you."

"Important? Obviously they're important. Why else would they be on the wall? I've been saving those for years. All the top jockeys. Bill Broughton. Jim Ellis. All their wins."

"I know," said Mum.

"Where has he put them?"

Mum's gaze slid to the fireplace. "They're in the firewood box, next to the coal range."

Sid rushed to the firewood box. "Well, I'm getting them out."

"He'll notice," said Mum.

"Let him notice. I don't care. Those are mine. He had no right to touch them."

Mum sighed. "It bothers him, Sid. The racing. He doesn't like it that you're so interested."

"I'll hide them." Sid scooped the newspaper cuttings up from where they had been dumped, then scrabbled through the wood box, searching for any that might have slipped down and hidden themselves among the lumps of wood. "At least he didn't screw them up. Or burn them. Yet."

"Look!" He held up a flimsy, faded piece of newsprint with a photograph. "Jim Ellis flying along – on his way to victory. And this one – Bill Broughton entering the birdcage."

"I know," said Mum.

Sid gathered them all and ran outside. Where could he hide them? The barn. Yes, hide them in the barn. But was that safe? Was anywhere safe, now that Dad was home?

Dinner was on the table when he came back in. His twin brothers, hair wet from the river, sat side by side. They looked like small, rumpled owls with their eyes big in their freckled faces and their sandy hair sticking up in all directions. He took his place next to his little sister, Ruby. "Hey, Rubes. Hungry?" He rubbed his tummy, raising his eyebrows. She nodded, grinning. Ruby was deaf. Infantile meningitis. Sid knew what those words meant.

"Here you go, Sid." Beryl, his older sister, handed him his plate. "Bangers and mash. Your favourite."

"It is, actually," said Sid, grabbing his knife and fork.

Beryl put on her sweetest voice. "Been out on Hugh, then? Practising your racing?"

"That'll do, Beryl." Mum straightened her apron. "Hugh's a good old horse for going across the paddocks and down to the river. You just leave Sid alone. He's allowed to dream." She frowned. "There's more than one dreamer around here. You let that fire go out, and you know we need hot water for the dishes. And as for your father..."

Sid and Beryl looked at each other. Yes, as for him... Mum said he was shell-shocked, but it just seemed like he hated everybody.

Sid was sure that his dad despised him, especially. He hardly ever spoke to him. He would sit behind his newspaper, but Sid could tell he wasn't reading it. He never turned a page. Then he'd suddenly dump the paper down, pick up his hat and stalk out of the house without a word.

He glanced at Dad's empty chair, at the head of the table. "Is Dad here for dinner?"

"He should be." Mum opened the door and peered out, then she picked up Dad's dinner and put it in the oven. "I'll keep it warm for him. Let's hope he comes home before it's all dried out."

Sid nodded. Privately, he hoped Dad wouldn't come back. At least, not until later, after they'd had their dinner in peace.

The war, far away, had ended on the second of September 1945. That was last year. Dad had returned from fighting in Crete. Sid's friend Rick had also got his dad back from fighting in the Pacific. Rick's dad seemed fine. He was behind the counter in the corner shop, weighing out flour and sugar like he'd never been away. Rick was lucky. His father seemed normal.

Sid ate fast, clearing his plate long before anyone else. He put it in the sink, then sidled towards the door. The evening was clear and fine, and there was plenty of time before bed.

"Hold your horses, Sidney Everett. Where are you going?"

Sid jumped. "Just outside, Mum."

"You did your homework after school, didn't you?"

"Yes."

"All of it?" asked Mum.

"Yes," said Sid.

"Wood brought in?"

Sid had no answer for that.

"Bring a load in, Sidney, before it gets dark." Mum bent and picked up Ruby, who was clinging to her skirt. "Come on Ruby, let's get you ready for bed." Ruby reached out an arm towards Sid and made a soft noise.

He crossed the floor and kissed her on the cheek. "Night night, Rubes." He rumpled her curls. "Sleep tight." He mimed an enormous yawn, patting his mouth. Ruby grinned. She waved to Sid over her mother's shoulder as she was carried off.

Sid picked up the wood bucket and headed for the door.

Outside, the evening was fresh and smelled of the forest. He paused for a moment. Crickets sang in the darkening garden, and a dog barked somewhere in the distance. The moon was a bright crescent in the deep blue of the eastern sky, rising above the ridge where spikes of pine trees stood up like the fur on the family dog when she was growling at something. Sid walked over to the woodpile and filled the wood bucket from the stack of split firewood, the lumps of dry wood tumbling brown and gold as they fell inside. He lugged the bucket into the house and dumped it into the woodbox beside the fire. Then he went back out for another load.

Old Hugh stamped and snuffled in his paddock over the fence. Sid could hear him munching grass. The warm smell of horse and dry grass drifted on the still air. Sid put down the bucket and slipped between the fence wires. He leaned against the horse and pressed the side of his face against Hugh's neck, breathing in the familiar horsey smell. "Poor old Hugh. You can't help being a plodder, can you?" Hugh dipped his head and chomped companionably. Sid lingered, watching the moon sail higher into the sky above the pine trees on the ridge.

"Sid!" Beryl's nearby voice made him jump. He spun around.

"Beryl, what are you doing out here?"

"Just looking at the moon. It's beautiful."

Sid glanced back up at the sky. "I suppose so." He climbed back through the fence, grabbed the wood bucket and filled it quickly, the lumps of wood clanging against the bucket as he threw them in, then he headed for the back door. Darkness was falling fast. Lamplight spilled out of the doorway and across the dirt path.

"Is Beryl out there?" Mum's voice sounded tired.

"Yeah," said Sid. "She's looking at the moon."

"She's dreaming again." Mum shook her head. "A family of dreamers."

"Don't worry, Mum." Sid grinned at his mother. "We've got our feet on the ground."

Mum smiled. "Thanks, Sid. Of course you have. You're all good kids. You never let me down, any of you, all through the war." She brushed a wisp of hair from her forehead. "Wash the dishes now, will you, Sid? There's a good boy. The twins can dry."

"Mum? Can I have a tin? For the newspaper cuttings."

"Of course you can, Sid." Mum reached up to a top cupboard. "I haven't done much baking lately. Plenty of empty tins." She handed Sid a round tin with a picture of a man and a woman in Victorian dress. "Mackintosh's Toffees. Is this one big enough?"

"Thanks, Mum." Sid hesitated. "Do you think he'll notice the cuttings are gone from the wood box?"

"I think he'll assume they've been burnt," said Mum. "I hope so. Or he might even have forgotten all about it. You just never know."

"All right, thanks Mum. I'll be back in a minute, and I'll wash the dishes."

"Good boy," said Mum. "Get them done. And if Dad comes in before you go to bed, you just clear off smartly. Don't say a word about anything. I don't want another row."

Chapter Two

Toheroa Season

Sid jumped awake, his eyes staring into darkness, his ears straining. Someone was moving around outside in the shed. The clang of a bucket and the sound of a wooden box scraping along a floor carried clearly on the night air. After years of his father being away, Sid's instinct to protect his mother and siblings was strong. He slept lightly and woke alert. He raised himself on one elbow level with the window and eased the curtain aside just enough to see out.

Lamplight was shining from the open shed doorway. Sid hunched up on the bed, peering out into the darkness. He saw the lanky silhouette of his father emerge, staggering a little, and begin then weaving its way up the path towards the house. Dad was carrying a lantern and bucket and something large was draped over his shoulder. The kitchen door banged, and Sid heard the murmur of voices. Voices that were getting louder. Mum and Dad arguing.

He slid down from the bed and crept across to the door.

"Sid!" One of the twins had woken. "Sid, what's happening?"

"Dunno. Dad brought a load of stuff in from the shed."

"What's the time?"

"I don't know," said Sid. "It feels like midnight."

Dad was shouting. Mum's footsteps approached along the hallway.

"Boys?" Mum opened the bedroom door. "Boys, your father wants everybody up." The light was behind her, so Sid couldn't see her face, but her voice was strained.

"Why, Mum?" he asked.

"Just get up, Sidney. Straight away. Bill? Bruce? Up you get. Your father wants you. I'm going to wake the girls."

Shivering, the family assembled in the kitchen. Sid and Beryl looked at each other. Ruby began to cry, and Beryl picked her up and held her close. The twins, wearing matching pyjamas, stood together with pinched faces. Only their eyes moved from Dad to Mum, following the conversation.

"Toheroa season!" Dad was bellowing. "It's toheroa season! Jack told me. We're meeting him on the beach." He glared around at his family as if waiting for someone to disagree. "It's the first day of the season. We'll be the first ones on the beach!"

Sid had always loved digging for the fat shellfish, his hands scooping sand as fast as they could as the toheroa dug deep, trying to escape. He'd been looking forward to the season, but he was pretty sure it wasn't starting yet. Not that he was going to argue. Things didn't seem normal right now. He didn't dare move, but his eyes met his mother's. She nodded almost imperceptibly. Did that mean it truly was toheroa season? Or did she just mean for them to go along with it?

He looked at Ruby, peeping from the safety of Beryl's arms, and mimed digging with his hands, then he formed the long oval of a toheroa.

Ruby whimpered. She started shaking her head, and her mouth turned down. Her eyes grew fearful. Last year, one of the giant shellfish had closed itself tight on her finger. Nobody had brought a knife, and without a knife, they couldn't open it. She cried all the way home, a toheroa grimly clamped on her little hand.

Dad roared, "Beryl! Let her stand on her own feet! She's not a baby!"

Beryl slid Ruby to the floor, where she stood shivering in her pyjamas, tears silently running down her cheeks.

Mum stepped forward. "Perhaps, my dear, it's best if Ruby doesn't go. She's only six years old..."

"I need everyone!" Dad towered over her. "Mary, you mollycoddle the child. She can get her quota like everyone else in this family. Everybody has to go. To get their quota."

"It's very dark, Arthur. It must be midnight."

"No, no. Nearly morning. Jack'll be there, waiting for us. We'll be the first ones on the beach. First ones..."

Sid glanced at the clock, its pale face glimmering in the moonlight. Half-past one. Nowhere near morning. Mum caught his eye and gave a faint shake of her head. Sid kept his mouth shut.

"It'll soon be light!" Dad swayed a little and waved his arm at a pile of brown sacks on the floor. "Grab one each, kids. And you, Mary. You need your own sack."

Nobody moved. Dad stooped slowly and picked up the sacks. He began handing them out. "Sidney. Beryl. Bruce. Bill. Ruby." The pile was gone. "Need two more. Two more. For me and Mother. Wait there."

Sid held his sack, feeling the rough hessian, smelling the warm smell of old potato sack. "This is real," he thought. Dad staggered back out into the darkness. Mum found a feather quilt and wrapped it around Ruby, who was shivering. Sid realised he was shivering, too. They all were. "Mum!" Sid looked at his mother. "Mum! This is crazy. It's dark outside! It's the middle of the night!"

"Your father thinks it's almost morning."

"It's half-past one, Mum. Nowhere near morning. Tell him, Mum!"

"I can't Sidney," said Mum. "He wouldn't listen. You can't reason with him when he's like this. Just go along with it, Sid."

"We can't walk to the beach in the middle of the night," said Sid. "And Jack, Mum! Crazy Jack!"

"I know," she said.

Sid knew Jack had come back from the war a bit strange. He wasn't called Crazy Jack for nothing. Everyone said he should be in a mental home.

"Jack's all right, Sid," said Mum. Mum sometimes seemed to understand exactly what he was thinking. "His wife looks after him. She won't have him sent away. It's the Māori way."

Jack sometimes joked that he should have fought in the Māori Battalion; he had so many Māori relatives. But Jack was Pākehā and he'd fought with Dad, and now they were best mates. Sid looked helplessly at his mother, her face a white blob in the shadowy kitchen. She must have sensed his gaze. "Just go along with it, Sidney. Wait and see what happens."

Sid watched the lantern bobbing around outside while the family stood like a group of statues in the dark room. The smell of the bush wafted in through the open door, and a morepork called in the distance. The clock ticked on the mantelpiece, louder than Mum's breathing or Ruby's sniffling.

Then, outside, there was an almighty crash, and the lantern went out. From the darkness, a string of low curses began. Dad's voice was getting louder and louder. They heard him yelling, heard something crashing again and again against the shed and the sound of glass smashing and tinkling.

"The window!" Mum rushed to the door. More smashing and crashing came from inside the shed. "My preserving jars!"

The crashing stopped. They could hear Dad's voice clearly now, roaring as he approached the house. "The door! Wouldn't open. Aaaaaahhh!!!" His voice stopped abruptly.

The only sound was the wind in the pine trees and then a soft thump.

"Arthur!" Mum rushed outside. She was back in a moment. "Dad's hurt. Help me, Sid. He's bleeding. He's lying on the path." She looked around the room, suddenly calm. Ruby had disappeared inside her quilt like a hedgehog rolled into a ball. "Beryl, take Ruby to bed and look after her. Bill and Bruce, back to bed." She paused, looking at their stricken faces. "Dad'll be all right. Don't worry, he'll be fine." She turned to Sid. "Sidney? Come with me."

***

Much later, Sid helped his mother into the rocking chair in the front room. "Are you sure you don't want me to stay?" he asked.

"I'll be fine, Sid. I'll keep watch," she said, pulling a blanket around herself. "You get some sleep."

"You too, Mum." He hesitated. "Mum? Is he going to be alright?" His eyes drifted to the unmoving form of his father. Dad lay on the sofa, eyes closed and head bandaged, snoring quietly. Sid's heart twisted as he looked down at his father's face.

"He will be, Sid." Mum blinked. "In the morning, he'll be alright. If he's not, I'll get the doctor. But I'm sure he'll be alright."

Sid turned away. Wearily, he trailed down the hallway to his bedroom and opened the door. Bill and Bruce were asleep, breathing steadily. A beam of moonlight shone through the half-open curtains, highlighting their tousled hair. He padded across the cold floorboards to bed. As he sank down, the door opened.

"Sid!" whispered Beryl.

"Beryl, are you still awake?"

"Of course I am." Beryl crossed the floor, a bulky shape wrapped in a thick eiderdown, her bare feet silent. The bed sagged as she sat on the end. "Sid, what happened?"

"Dunno, really," said Sid. "Dad was trying to open the shed door, the one that's nailed shut. He must have forgotten it was nailed. He smashed it open—bashed it open with the milk bucket. And when he got inside, he started smashing everything." Sid paused. "The bucket's not much good anymore."

"Nor are Mum's jars, by the sound of it." Beryl giggled and then stopped. "I don't know why I'm laughing. Sid, I'm scared. What if he's going crazy?"

"Yeah," said Sid. "I know what you mean. But Mum thinks he'll be all right." He wished his voice sounded a little less doubtful. "Beryl, if you saw his face, like he is just now, asleep, you'd feel, I dunno, like he's just a little boy, and we need to look after him." Sid shook his head. "Nah. Don't worry, Beryl. Mum would do something if he was going crazy. She'd get a doctor."

"Yeah, I suppose so," said Beryl. She shifted on the bed, tugging the eiderdown up around her shoulders. "Sid? Is it really toheroa season? Mum hasn't said anything about it."

"Could be," he answered. "It's that time of the year."

"Is Dad in bed?" she asked.

"He's lying on the sofa," said Sid. "Mum's keeping watch."

"Oh, well. That's good, I suppose." Beryl hesitated. "Sid?"

"Yeah?"

"Thanks for looking after him."

"Looking after him?" he said.

"Helping Mum," said Beryl. "You always help."

Sid felt a bit awkward. "That's all right, Beryl. I do what I can. While I'm still here."

"What do you mean, while you're still here?" Beryl's voice sounded suspicious.

"Well, you know I need an apprenticeship. To be a jockey." His heart beat faster. "Actually, I can't wait to get away from here. With Dad like he is. Especially after tonight. I have to find somewhere that'll take me on, that's all."

"Oh. Yeah, the jockey thing. Well, don't rush. It's getting scary here." She got up. "Night, Sid!"

"Good night, Beryl." Sid grinned in the darkness. "Sleep well."

Sometime towards morning, Sid woke again to the soft notes of a harmonica. The strains of Somewhere Over the Rainbow drifted up from below. Dad was playing his favourite tune, and that meant he was happy. Although Sid knew it didn't mean he'd still be happy by the time the sun rose. He looked over at the dark shapes of his brothers, sound asleep. Lucky them. He tugged his quilt further up around his shoulders and snuggled down. He wasn't looking forward to the morning.

Chapter Three

School

"See you later, Hugh." Sid turned his horse out into the paddock next to the school. He checked that there was water in the trough and clicked the gate shut. It was very quiet. Skylarks sang somewhere high overhead, and magpies warbled in the distance. There was no sound of children's voices. He saw that the playground was empty.

Late again. He cursed the cause of his lateness - the two cows he had to milk every morning. He had tried reasoning with his mother.

"Mum, what's the point? We don't need that much milk!"

"I need the cream cheques, Sidney. I don't know how we'd manage without the cream money. The cows are staying, and you're milking them!"

A sudden sense that he was being watched made him look around. Next to the big tōtara by the gate, a man was standing. Crazy Jack. And stepping out from the shadow of the tree, a small, dark woman and two tall young men. Jack's sons. He hadn't seen them since they'd finished school a couple of years ago.

"Good morning, Sid." Jack's voice was raspy.

"Hello, Jack." Scenes from last night flashed through Sid's mind. He narrowed his eyes at his dad's drinking partner.

"Thought I'd catch you before school," said Jack.

Sid glanced across at the school. "I'm a bit late," he muttered.

Jack stepped closer. "I need to talk to you, Sidney. Need to tell you something. 'Bout your father..."

"About my father?" Sid felt his cheeks burn, and he couldn't keep an angry edge out of his voice. He fixed his eyes on Hugh, grazing nearby. "We didn't get much sleep at our place last night. Toheroa season?"

"I'm sorry about that, Sid. I tried to stop him. He had the wrong end of the stick. I knew he did." Jack squeezed his eyes shut, then opened them again. They were a bright, light blue. "I told him that we should be first on the beach when the season starts. But he didn't listen properly. He thought I meant now. And once he got the idea into his head, he wouldn't listen to another thing."

"No?" Sid looked up, reluctantly. He could see the purple lines in Jack's red cheeks, the grey pouches under his eyes. He glanced at Jack's wife and she gave him a quick, sympathetic smile. Her sons stood like dark wooden statues. Sid sensed that they were sort of protecting their mother. And Jack.

Jack noticed his gaze. "You remember my sons? Peter. James. At school with you?"

"Yes," said Sid.

The young men looked at Sid, acknowledging him with a slight lift of their chins. They'd been seniors a couple of years ago. And now—now they were men.

"But that's not why I'm here," Jack continued. "Toheroa season's nothing. Neither here nor there. I'm talking about the man himself. Arthur Everett. Your father." Jack paused and closed his eyes again, as if he was trying hard to find the right words. Sid waited. Then the bright blue eyes snapped open, staring into his. "This is what I want to say. Don't worry about your father, Sid. He's a good man. He risked his life for me in the war. I'd trust Arthur Everett with my life, time and again. Anywhere. No matter what." He cleared his throat. "My wife has something to say. She had a dream." He looked back at his wife and jerked his head towards Sid.

Jack's wife stepped forward, her small figure calm and dignified. She stood for a moment with her hands clasped together, a sort of far-away remembering look on her face. Then she took a deep breath, straightened her shoulders and her eyes met Sid's. "I saw your father. I could hear waves crashing. And it was dark."

Sid stared. "What...?"

Jack broke in. "It's the matakite, Sid. The second sight. She can see things sometimes."

His wife continued. "I heard waves crashing in the darkness. But your father—his face! He was like a man who..." She paused, searching for words. "Who won a tremendous victory. His face was shining."

She looked up at her husband with a questioning expression, and then turned back to Sid, reaching out a hand to touch his arm. She smiled reassuringly. "There you are," she said.

"Well, that's it," said Jack. He put his face so close to Sid's that he could feel his hot breath and smell the stale beer. "Don't you worry about your father, Sid. Just give him time. He'll come right. That's what we want to say. He'll come right."

Sid froze. It was like a prophecy, a fortune teller's words. He blinked, trying to break the spell. "Um, thanks, Jack. Yeah, he's good, my dad, yeah." He backed away. "See you later, Jack. I've gotta go." He turned and bolted into the school playing field.

The wet grass was cold and slippery under Sid's bare feet, and sticky paspalum seed heads flicked against his legs. He slowed to a walk. No point in running. He looked back. Jack and his family, a small group, were already distant on the road.

Sid slipped into the gloom of the school building. He breathed in the familiar smell of paint and chalk dust that always made him long for the outdoors. As he passed the closed door of the junior class, he could hear them chanting their times tables. Miss Heatherton was doing the daily drill. Back when Sid had been in the junior class, he'd suffered old Mrs Taylor with her stiff grey hair and fierce eyes.

Terrifying. Lucky primers now, to have Miss Heatherton.

Sid hung his leather satchel in the cloakroom and opened the door to the senior class.

"Afternoon, Sidney," said Mr Cowley.

"Sorry I'm late, sir," said Sid. He hurried to his desk.

Mr Cowley gave him a dark look from under his bushy eyebrows, but said nothing more.

Sid took his place next to his friend Rick, who gave him a grin. A hiss came from behind him. "Late again, Everett." It was Roger Dyson, of course.

Ignoring Roger, he lifted the lid of his desk and slipped his books inside. His eyes had already taken in the form of his sister Beryl sitting on the far side of the room beside her friend Glenys. Beryl got a ride to school every day with Glenys, and Glenys was never late. Sid also noted Sarah Thorndon, sitting just behind Beryl.

Sarah Thorndon. Sid didn't look at her directly, but his peripheral vision captured her in an instant. She sat straight-backed, her fair hair shining in the light from the high windows. Knowing she was in the classroom made everything else in the day seem worthwhile.

Sarah was the only daughter of Mr Gerald Thorndon, owner of Thorndon racing stables and Sid's family's only near neighbour. But although the Thorndon estate and the Everett's rented ten-acre block were adjacent, the two families were socially worlds apart. Sid sighed and forced his attention back to the front of the room.

"As I was saying…" Mr Cowley shot Sid another look, "some of you will be contemplating your futures. Possibly. Most of you are probably thinking no further ahead than lunchtime. Hmm?" He looked around the room. "Life is longer than a day at school. Longer than childhood."

Mr Cowley picked up his pointing stick. It was long and made of wood, like a slender billiard cue. Its purpose was to draw attention to items on the blackboard, but Mr Cowley mostly used it as something to twirl as he talked.

Sid's gaze followed the pointer as his teacher's fingertips made it spin slowly in the air. Mr Cowley was as good as a major in a pipe band. Sid appreciated his skill, although he couldn't help hoping his teacher would fumble and the pointer would spiral out of control and crash to the floor.

Mr Cowley continued. "You have your lives ahead of you. Your futures to consider. The government…" He paused. "No, forget the government. I'll save that hobby horse. We're talking about work. About our futures. Hands up, those who know what they want to do after finishing school."

Beryl's hand shot up.

"Yes, Beryl?"

"I want to be a teacher, sir."

"A primary school teacher? Or secondary?"

"Primary, sir," said Beryl. "Like Miss Heatherton."

"Excellent, Beryl. You'd make a wonderful teacher. Now, I've got a question for you." Mr Cowley looked around the room. "Knowing your goal is one thing. That's the first step. How to get there is much harder." He looked at Beryl again. "So, Miss Beryl, tell us, how does one become a teacher?"

"You go to Teachers' Training College, sir," she said.

"Good. And have you thought about which training college you'll go to?"

"Well..." Beryl paused, unused to so much attention. Her cheeks were pink. "I could go to the Collegiate, sir. Unless..."

"Yes?" he asked.

"I might go away somewhere. Somewhere different. Somewhere a lot bigger than Foxton. Like Christchurch. Or Auckland."

"Youthful adventure, eh?"

Beryl's cheeks flushed even pinker.

"I didn't mean to embarrass you, Beryl." Mr Cowley smiled. "It's an excellent plan." He glanced around the room. "Anyone else?"

The class was silent.

"Sidney?"

Sid jumped. "Yes, sir?"

"See me at interval."

Heads turned to look at Sid. He sat upright at his wooden desk, ignoring their gaze, his eyes on Mr Cowley.

"Yes, sir," he said.

"All right, everyone." Mr Cowley shouldered his pointing stick like a rifle. "Take out your homework."

Desk lids raised and banged down again; books flapped open.

"In trouble, are we, Everett?" a low voice murmured behind him.

"Shut up, Dyson," Sid snapped.

Sid laid a battered exercise book on his desk and opened it at last night's page of sums. His eyes, however, didn't take in his neatly pencilled figures. He saw instead a horse and rider flying along the track, a cheering crowd, and his name in the newspaper headlines: SIDNEY EVERETT WINS AGAIN!'

Before dismissing the class at playtime, Mr Cowley got one of the girls to hand out apples. It was a new thing, since the war ended. Sid took his and stuffed it into his pocket. As the other students filed out of the room, he waited by the teacher's desk.

He felt the curious stares of his classmates burning the back of his neck as they passed him. Surely he wasn't in trouble for being late? He was always late. It was his normal start to the day.

"Now, Sidney, I want a word with you before you set off into life," Mr Cowley said.

"Sir?," said Sid.

"You missed the beginning of my little talk this morning. Now pay attention, this is important. You're almost fifteen, and I believe your parents expect you to leave school as soon as you can. Money's tight, I know. It's the same for many families around here." Mr Cowley considered Sid, his bushy eyebrows raised. "Think hard before you leave, Sidney. You have great potential. You're bright, you're sharp. You could go far." He paused. "Do you know what you'd like to do?"

Sid hesitated. His dream of being a famous jockey seemed too personal to share aloud. "I don't know, sir."

Mr Cowley eyed him. "I know you're keen on horses. I used to see you racing along the beach." He paused. "Well?"

"Sir?"

"Well, you like riding. You're built like a jockey. You're not interested in the racing world, by any chance?"

Sid stared. "Well, yes. I am," he admitted. "But my dad doesn't like racing."

"I see. Since the war?"

"No. Before then." Sid felt relieved to talk about it. "We used to go to the races a lot, with Rick's family. Then he just suddenly changed." He frowned. "We stopped going. And my dad is dead set against racing now. He doesn't like me talking about it. And he won't let me go to the races with Rick's family anymore."

"Well, some people are against racing," said Mr Cowley. "But you say he used to take you all?"

"Yes, sir. Our whole family used to go."

"Hmm." Mr Cowley frowned. "Well, Sidney, I want you to consider staying on at school. Education's the thing. You need to keep on with your education. If you leave at fifteen, there's not a lot out there for you. Farm work. Road work. Building dams. We're always building dams in this country."

Sid squirmed, but kept his mouth shut.

Mr Cowley sighed. "Not what you'd choose, of course. But you need to think ahead. It's very likely that you'll end up doing that sort of work if you don't have a *plan*. It's what's called a *default* option." He eyed Sid. "Do you know what *default* means?"

"It's when people can't pay their debts, sir."

"Yes, that's one meaning. But in this case..." Mr Cowley wrote with chalk on the blackboard, in his neat cursive writing. Default. "In this case," he tapped the word, "it means that thing you slip into doing, if nothing else has been planned or organised."

Sid stood in silence.

"For example," Mr Cowley continued, "I have noticed that playing marbles is the default option for many in this school, given a bit of free time."

Sid allowed himself a small smile.

"I'm appealing to you, Sidney," said Mr Cowley. "Think before you leap. Education is the key to a better future. It's free, and it's your ticket to a significant life. You might be somebody."

Sid felt the hair on his head prickle. It seemed like the teacher was using his very own words.

"You're a fine boy, Sidney. I know you took good care of your mother while your dad was away. But now... Now there'll be pressure on you to quit school as soon as you can. To get a job. Any job." The eyebrows came together. "Don't do it. Stay at school." Mr Cowley gave him a quiet, almost apologetic smile. "All right, Sidney. Sermon's over. Off you go."

***

Outside in the bright sunlight, Sid searched for Rick. He found him in the centre of a bunch of older students. Rick was head-to-head with Roger Dyson, his face bright red.

"You think you own everything, Dyson," snarled Rick.

"Well, my father does own a lot of property around here." Roger raised his eyebrows. "Including a certain block of shops in town. Your father leases the corner shop, I think?"

Sid grabbed Rick's arm. "Rick! Leave it!"

Rick shook him off. "Just a minute, Sid." He turned back to Roger. "That's none of your business, Dyson. At least my father went off to fight in the war. What was your dad doing while the war was on? Making sure my mum paid the rent on the shop?"

"Rick!" Sid punched his friend in the side. "Come on. Let's go."

Roger smirked at Sid. "Oh, Everett. Finished your little chat with the teacher? What did old Cowley want? Did he give you five hundred lines? 'I must not be late for school'?"

"Actually, it was 'I must not talk to pompous fools.'"

"I suppose he gave you a little talk about what to do when you turn fifteen?"

Sid stiffened, and Roger laughed, seeing that he was right.

"I should say you've got your future all cut out for you, Sid," he said. "No need to think about it. Plenty of labouring work around."

Sid flushed. "I have my plans, Dyson, but they're none of your business."

Roger laughed. "I'm sure you have your little plans, Everett. Hope you won't be too disappointed."

Sid's hands clenched into fists. He'd show Roger. One day, his name would be famous. He turned the talk away from himself. "What are you going to do, Dyson?"

"Oh, I'll join my father in his business, I suppose. Once I finish university." Roger smirked.

A group of girls approached, Sarah in the centre. Roger stepped out from the bunch of boys.

"Good morning, Sarah," he said.

"Morning, Roger." Sarah grinned.

Sid could hear Rick making gagging noises next to him.

"We were just discussing the future, Sarah." Roger stepped closer to her. "I suppose you'll be off to university?"

Sarah looked at Roger, puzzled, then at Rick and Sid. "I suppose so. Not that I've decided what to study."

Sid noticed, close up, that Sarah still had a few freckles on her nose. When she was younger, she'd had lots of freckles. She murmured something to the other girls, and they all giggled. She turned back to Roger. "Actually, I'm sick of all this 'what are you going to do?' Dad's been nagging me to decide. What's the rush?" She swept away, followed by her friends, her fair hair bouncing as she walked.

Roger grinned triumphantly. "Lovely girl, that Sarah. I wonder which university she'll go to?"

Sid glared. Some people seemed to have a red carpet rolled out ahead of them. All they had to do was step on it and start walking. His own road would be made of racing turf, if he had his way. Although at the moment, all he could see was a mountain of obstacles ahead.

"Come on, Sid." Rick elbowed him. "Sarah knows a show-off when she sees one." He narrowed his eyes at Roger. "She's not impressed by swank!"

As they walked away, Rick grabbed Sid's arm. "Hey, I just remembered. Mum said, do you want to come to the races with us? On Saturday."

Sid grinned in amazement. "You bet!" He frowned. "I can't tell Dad where I'm going. He'd never let me go."

"Just tell him we're going to Wanganui," said Rick.

"I can't lie," said Sid.

"It's not lying," said Rick. "We are going to Wanganui. You don't need to say it's to the races."

"Nah," said Sid. "I won't tell him anything. He'd ask questions. He'd want to know why we're going. I'll ask Mum - she'll say yes. And she won't mention it to Dad."

The bell rang for class to resume. No time for marbles. But Sid didn't care. Marbles was a kid's game. He sensed that his time for playing marbles was just about over.

Chapter Four

Racetrack

"Lovely to have you with us, Sidney." Rick's mum beamed at Sid across the picnic blanket. "It's been such a long time since you came to the races with us!" She offered him a plate of scones, each one spread with butter and topped with a dollop of raspberry jam. "Go on. Have one."

"Thanks, Mrs Cunningham." Sid took a scone.

She sighed. "Your family always used to join us. Those were good times—your family and ours." She smiled. "Do you remember that day when you were a little boy, and you told everyone you were going to be a jockey? The day Bill Broughton won the Central Cup?"

Sid nodded. "Yes, I remember." He also remembered, but didn't mention, that that was the day his father had stopped the family from going to the races.

"The boy's too keen on racing by far. You heard him, Mother. 'I'm going to be a jockey when I grow up.' Well, he isn't."

"He's very young, Arthur. He'll most likely change his mind and want to be a policeman. Or a fireman. You know how boys are. And then he'll probably end up doing something completely different."

"I'm not risking it. No more race-going for this family."

Rick's mum continued. "Yes, it was the day Bill Broughton won the Cup. I'll never forget it. You were so excited!"

Rick's family still often went to the races, mostly in Foxton. But the Everett family had never joined them again. Today, Sid hadn't asked permission from his dad. He knew Dad would say 'no'. Mum had whispered 'yes' and Sid had crept out early, hoping his father wouldn't find out where he'd gone. He breathed in the exhilarating aromas of the day. Fresh turf, horses and home baking. Bliss! He took a gigantic bite of his scone.

Although it was early, the grassy area near the racetrack was crowded with punters, all dressed in their best. Rick's dad was wearing his race day jacket and a new-looking hat. Mrs Cunningham was squeezed into a flowery cotton dress and she wore a green felt hat on her head, held in place by a massive pearly hat pin. Her face and neck were already pink from the heat. She pulled off her cardigan and folded it carefully before stowing it in her very large handbag.

"Brew's ready," she said to her husband. "Pot of tea, nice and hot. Want a cup?"

Rick caught Sid's eye. "Eat up," he whispered. "I want to walk around." Sid and Rick finished their scones and stood up. Rick looked at his mother. "Mum, we're going for a walk."

His younger sister Jeannie jumped up. "Can I come?"

"No, you stay here with Mum," said Rick. "We might be a long time."

"Yes, you stay with us, Jeannie." Rick's mum smoothed out the picnic blanket. "And sit back down on the blanket. Keep your dress nice and clean."

Rick elbowed Sid. "Come on, let's go."

The boys strolled off. Sid glanced back and saw Jeannie gazing after them. "You could have let her come, Rick."

"Nah! She'd slow us down. I want to go over to where they're walking the horses around. If Jeannie was with us, we'd get told to clear off. But just us, we might even get asked to help with something."

The area between the stables and the track was marked No Public Admittance. Sid and Rick sauntered in anyway, hoping that if they looked confident, nobody would challenge them. It worked. They wandered over to a chestnut thoroughbred tied to a railing. Sid stroked the shining neck.

"Different to old Hugh, eh?" Rick grinned at him.

"Yeah, rather different." Sid put his face close to the horse and breathed in the smell of oiled leather and warm horse.

"Hey you boys, get away from that horse," a man called to them.

"Sorry, mister. Just admiring him," said Rick.

Another groom was walking a large black horse. Sid walked alongside.

"You supposed to be in here?" The groom eyed Sid.

"Well, no," said Sid.

"Like horses, do you?"

"Yup." Sid reached an arm up and stroked the horse's neck. The groom slowed and halted, then led the black over to a rail and tied him there. "I'll be back in a minute. You can talk to him if you want. I can tell he likes you." He ran off. Sid stroked the horse's neck and rubbed his finger along the shiny leather of the halter.

Rick joined him, grinning. "You look the part all right, Sid. You look like you've been doing this all your life."

"Yeah, well, I have. On the farm." Sid gazed around, still stroking the horse's neck. "But it's a bit different here."

"Thanks, son." The groom returned, untied the horse and started walking him up and down again.

Sid followed. "What's his name?"

"Beach Dancer," said the groom.

"Beach Dancer! Nice name," said Sid. "Do you ride him on the beach?"

"Sometimes," said the man.

"I used to ride my horse on the beach," said Sid. "When he was younger."

"Horses love the beach. And it's good for them." The man looked at Sid and Rick. "Better get out of here, boys." He pointed to the sign. "*No Public Admittance*, see?"

Sid and Rick made their way back to the trackside. Sid elbowed his friend. "Did you hear that, Rick? Horses like the beach. Well, I knew that. And it's good for them."

Rick scowled. "Not fair, getting kicked out."

"Oh, well." Sid wasn't worried. "We had a look. C'mon, races are starting!"

"Just in time, boys." Mrs Cunningham flapped her hands at the folded picnic blanket and the baskets. "Grab something. Put it all back in the car. The first race is about to start!"

Rick picked up the two baskets. Sid picked up the wooden beer crate with the billy, the teapot, and all the cups, and Rick's mum laid the picnic blanket over the top.

"Come back here, son, when you've put everything in the car." Mr Cunningham spoke absently, his mind on the line-up for the first race. "We aren't going into the stand. We'll be by the rail."

***

"Oops! Excuse me!" Sid dodged first one way and then another, trying to get past a smartly dressed gentleman with binoculars hanging around his neck.

"Not at all, young man. Have to allow for a young jockey."

"Thank you, sir." Sid hesitated. "Actually, I'm not a jockey. I'm just here to watch the races."

"Not a jockey, eh?" The gentleman peered at Sid. "You certainly look like one. But now I see that's a picnic blanket you've got there, not a horse blanket." He tilted his head to one side. "Could be a jockey, though. Right weight, right build. Eh, Gerald?" He turned to the man next to him. Sid gulped. It was Mr Thorndon, Sarah's father.

"Yes, indeed." Mr Thorndon smiled. "Hello, young Sidney. Haven't seen you for a while. You always had your eyes set on riding a winner, didn't you? You used to tell us that when you were a lad."

Sid gulped again. "Um, well," he stammered, "yes sir. I still want to do that."

"Hmmm. Well, we're not hiring at the moment, of course. And you're still at school. But who knows what the future may hold?" Mr Thorndon nodded. "Good luck to you, boy."The two men walked on.

Sid turned to Rick. He could have jumped for joy if there weren't so many people around and if he wasn't carrying a heavy crate. "Did you hear that, Rick? It's what I want. It's exactly what I want!"

"Hear what? He didn't offer you anything," said Rick.

"Well, no, I suppose not. He didn't actually offer anything," said Sid. "But he was sort of positive."

They continued on their way to the car, Sid's mind in a whirl.

Not hiring right now? But of course, sometimes they were hiring. Who knows what the future may hold, Mr Thorndon had said. Those were his very words.

"Next year, Rick!" said Sid. "When I've finished school, I'll ask him for sure!"

He and Rick stuffed all the picnic gear into the boot of the car, then sped back to the track, ready for the first race. They had just reached the edge of the crowd when Rick spotted something on the ground.

"Sid. Wait." He picked up a tightly folded paper. "Look! A betting slip!"

Sid peered at the ticket in his friend's hand. "Hey! It's for Beach Dancer! Somebody must have just dropped it." He gazed around at the crowds. "It could have been anyone. So many people here."

"What race is it for?" said Rick. "Let's show Dad."

Mr Cunningham held the ticket out at arm's length and squinted at it. "It's for just one race. Beach Dancer. 11:15. Odds are six to one. Four shillings to win." He looked at the boys. "Where did you find it?"

"Just on the grass." Rick was grinning all over his face. "Can I keep it?"

"Not much else you can do," said his dad. "If you hold it up and ask if anyone dropped it, a hundred people will say yes."

Mrs Cunningham laughed. "That's for sure! Maybe it's your lucky day, Ricky boy."

"I'll split it with Sid, if the horse wins," said Rick.

"Really? Thanks, Rick," said Sid. "You know, I can't believe it's for Beach Dancer. That's amazing."

"Yeah, it is." Rick turned to his mother. "Mum, that's the horse we just saw over in, uh, we just saw. Being walked around. He was called Beach Dancer."

"Well, that's lucky too," she said. "Definitely."

Sid and Rick squeezed in next to Rick's parents, right up at the front, against the rail. Sid could feel the solid, sweating mass of the crowd pressing behind him. The microphone crackled, and the familiar but hard-to-understand language of the racetrack filled the air. They had a perfect view of the line-up. Sid stared at the racehorses. Some stamped and snorted, others were quiet. But each one was alert, ready for the start. A hush fell, then the loud crack of the starter rang out, and the race began.

The ground shuddered, and Sid felt a rush of excitement as the roar of the crowd filled his ears. The horses thundered past in a dazzle of speed and colour. Mrs Cunningham's sturdy bulk pressed against his shoulder, her voice shrill in his ears. Sid leaned out, his eyes following the gleaming horses with their bright colours, the jockeys bent low. Around the track they flew again, hooves pounding. The roar of the crowd became deafening now as the horses neared the finish line. Chunks of turf flew up into the air as they flashed past and over the line.

The Cunninghams bent over their betting slips, shaking their heads.

"Race two, Dad," said Rick. "Wait for race two. That's the lucky race, eh, Sid?"

Sid couldn't speak. His mouth was dry. He felt almost as if he was in a dream, with the smell of the turf and the crowd jostling. The charged atmosphere made his head spin, and the ticket in Rick's hand was like, well, miraculous. It was such a lucky find - they couldn't possibly have found it for no reason.

"Oh, well. I suppose we've got a long, boring wait now, until the next race," said Rick. "Shall we go back to the groom's area?" he whispered.

"No, they'd chuck us out for sure," said Sid.

Mrs Cunningham took Jeannie by the hand and began to lead her away through the crowd. "It won't be too long to wait," she called back. "I'll just find a bit of shade. Come on, Jeannie."

***

Eventually, the loudspeaker crackled back into life, announcing the next race. Sid and Rick rejoined the Cunningham family at the rail as the horses were led out for the second race.

"There he is, Mr Cunningham." Sid pointed. "Beach Dancer. Number eight. He's black, and his rider's wearing green and gold."

"He's a good-looking horse." Mr Cunningham stabbed a finger onto his own betting slip. "I've put two bob on number three, Hideaway, each way. That means either a win or a place. She's the favourite. Most likely to win, but she'll pay out less than Beach Dancer would."

The horses were lining up. Sid could see that Beach Dancer was dancing around a bit. He was just like his name.

Mr Cunningham continued. "If your ticket was for Queenie Girl, see, number eleven, and she won, she'd pay sixteen to one. Generous odds, because she always comes in near the end. You'd make a packet off Queenie Girl, if she actually won."

Sid nodded. "So, Beach Dancer, at six to one, he's somewhere in the middle?"

"Yes, that's right." Mr Cunningham nodded. "Look. They're about ready, now."

"And they're off... with Likely Lad in the lead, Mystery Girl coming on close behind and there's Lady Alma making her move, Hideaway coming up on the outside, and Beach Dancer moving up to fourth place... "

Sid struggled to follow the commentary. The words tumbled into his ears so rapidly, and the names of the horses were confusing. But Beach Dancer was moving up to fourth place. He had heard that clearly enough. And he could see that Beach Dancer was right up in the front bunch of horses.

The horses were around the other side of the track now - a fast-moving blur of colour. One or two were straggling behind, and he couldn't see Beach Dancer at all. He must still be in the front, somewhere where the horses were bunched together. The commentary was so crackly and fast, he couldn't follow it at all. The race rounded the curve at the bottom of the track, and he saw his horse again, a fast-moving black blur, and the flash of green and gold of the jockey's silks. Somewhere near the front. But not very near. More in the middle of the race, really. Then they were coming up the home straight. He tuned his ears to the commentary again.

"And Hideaway leading the field with Lady Alma coming up behind, Mystery Girl in third place, and Black Diamond fourth and First Water coming up on the outside now, Daybreak on the inside, dropping back, Likely Lad moving up, and now we see Beach Dancer coming up on the outside, Beach Dancer moving up into third place, Beach Dancer gaining, Lady Alma in second and Mystery Girl in fourth, Hideaway still leading..."

The horses were thundering past now, right in front of them, a blur of muscle and gleaming coats straining for the win. The jockeys were crouched low, putting all their concentration and energy into this last, crucial part of the race.

"And Beach Dancer moving up, and we have Black Diamond and Hideaway neck and neck, and Lady Alma dropping back and it's Mystery Girl in second place and Beach Dancer moving right up into first..."

The crowd was roaring, and Sid yelled along with the rest. So did Rick, beside him. And suddenly it was over. The commentator was announcing clearly, and more slowly, the winner. Beach Dancer, by a length, followed by Hideaway in second place and Mystery Girl in third.

Sid was breathing hard. He and Rick looked at each other and just laughed out loud. Rick's dad was wiping the sweat off his face, and he was laughing, too. "Well, boys, a lucky day for you." He looked down at his betting slip. "At least I'll get something for a place. Mine came in second. But yours! Well done, boys!"

Later, his hands trembling slightly, Sid received his winnings. Rick's dad had gone up and presented the ticket. It had paid out twenty-four shillings, plus the four shilling stake back again, which made twenty-eight shillings in all. Sid clutched a ten-shilling note and four silver coins. More money than he'd ever had in his whole life.

"Ricky, my boy, that money is going straight into the Post Office," said Rick's mother. "You have to save the lot of it." She turned to Sid. "What about you, Sidney? Saving yours too?"

"I think I'll give it to my mum, Mrs Cunningham." He turned to Rick. "If you're sure, Rick? To let me have half?"

"Of course," said Rick.

"Well, thank you. I'll give it to Mum." He grinned. "It'll end up in your shop, anyway. I just have to make sure I keep it quiet. You know. From Dad. I don't know what he'd say if he knew I'd been to the races today, let alone winning some money!"

***

"Mum. I've got something for you." Sid held out the ten-shilling note. Then he opened his other hand and showed her the coins.

"Sid! Fourteen shillings. I can't believe it!" She glanced around. "Quick. Hide it away. But where..?" Her voice grew stern. "Not the races? You didn't bet?" She frowned. "Sidney, I hope you never placed a bet."

"Nah. Of course not. Didn't have any money, anyway." Sid couldn't help laughing—his mother looked so amazed. "And I wouldn't waste it on betting, if I did."

"Well, how on earth...?"

"Rick found a ticket," said Sid. "On the ground. And he split the winnings with me." Sid pressed the money into his mother's hand. "It's for you. Honestly, Mum, it was unbelievable luck!"

"Sid, isn't that like... stealing?"

"How can it be? The crowds, Mum. You know what it's like. How could we possibly find out whose ticket it was? If we asked if somebody had lost a ticket, every man there would've put his hand up."

"I suppose you're right." She looked at the money. "Fourteen shillings! Oh, Sid, you can't think how worried I've been about money."

"I think I know." He closed her fingers over the money. "Here. Put it away." He kissed her on the cheek. "Maybe it's an omen? Good luck coming our way?"

"What's that?" Dad's voice boomed from the doorway, making Sid and his mother jump. "Good luck coming our way? Fat chance."

He swung the door shut behind him and then stopped as he took in the frozen figures of his wife and son. "What's going on here?"

"Sidney." Mum's voice was suddenly faint. "Nip out and get the firewood in. Before it gets dark."

Sid grabbed the wood bucket and headed out into the dusk, his heart hammering with shock and dismay. The money would soon be in Dad's hands, he knew. And he was in trouble, for sure.

Chapter Five

Hard Times

Sid crouched in the woodshed, legs cramped, listening to his parents' raised voices back in the house, to banging doors, Ruby crying, and eventually silence. Jess, the family dog, came and found him. He stroked her head, grateful for the company. By the time he came in with the firewood, the kitchen was empty, his parents in their bedroom, and the house in darkness. He scanned the kitchen for something to eat. Maybe in the oven? Yes, a plate of dinner. Shepherd's pie, still warm. He wolfed it down, rinsed his plate in the sink and crept off to bed. It just wasn't fair. Nothing was fair.

"Next time I have any money," he muttered, "I'll bury it."

***

The next morning, he hurried out early to milk the cows, avoiding the family. Beryl was waiting at the back door when he returned with the milk.

"Sid. Leave the milk. Dad wants to talk to you." She lowered her voice. "Watch out, he's in a mood."

"I bet he is. Okay, I'm coming."

At the kitchen table, the twins were putting milk and golden syrup on their porridge. Dad was in the kitchen corner, on the wooden bench seat. He was humming a tune, acting like he was happy. His tobacco tin lay on the scrubbed surface of the table, the inside of the open lid reflecting golden sunlight. The sweet smell of tobacco mingled with the smell of wood smoke and porridge in the small room. Sid stood and watched as his dad rolled a thin cigarette, carefully placing it on the table next to the tin.

"Sidney?" said Dad. "What's this I hear about horse racing?"

Sid jumped, although he'd been expecting this. "Horse racing, Dad?"

"You know what I'm talking about. With the Cunninghams. Yesterday."

"Oh, that. Yes, they took me with them," said Sid.

"And you won some money."

"I didn't win it. Rick won it. With a ticket he found." Sid narrowed his eyes. "And I gave it to Mum."

"Well, she knows what's best for the family. Safest in my keeping," said Dad.

Sid doubted that, but he didn't speak.

"Got anything to say about that?" Dad's face hardened as he waited for Sid's response.

"I just wanted to help Mum," he said.

"You just wanted to have some fun. The money was luck. Helping Mum was an afterthought."

"It was my first thought!" said Sid.

"Don't answer back!" Dad always had to have the final word. Sid kept his mouth shut and waited.

"Now." His father had his most serious face on. "You knew I didn't want you at the races. You deliberately disobeyed my wishes. That's the first thing. And you were being deceptive. That's the second thing."

Sid bit his lip, wishing Dad would get to the point.

"And another thing," said Dad. "The twins are telling me you're going to be a famous jockey."

Sid stared. "Oh, that. Oh, they get these ideas..." He flicked a quick glare at Bill and Bruce, eating porridge at the other end of the table.

Dad pulled himself up straighter in his seat. "You're almost fifteen, Sidney. Getting to be a man. Soon be earning a man's wage, eh?"

"Uh, yes." Sid thought of Mr Cowley with his bushy eyebrows and piercing eyes. He took a deep breath. "Mr Cowley thinks I should stay at school, Dad. Get a better education."

"Does he really?" said Dad. "And I suppose he knows where his next meal's coming from. Which is more than many families around here can be sure of."

Sid made up his mind. He didn't want more education, anyway. "Dad, I don't want to stay on at school. I want to train as a jockey." The words rushed out faster than he'd meant them to. "I could be an apprentice. Mr Thorndon takes on apprentice jockeys. There's money in racing. And sometimes, you can get... famous." He glanced at his father's face.

"And how much do they pay apprentices?" Dad asked.

"I don't know." Sid considered. "I suppose you get your board, and a bit of a wage. But once you're actually a jockey..."

"Sidney, listen to me." Dad gazed at the unlit cigarette for a long time. His eyes were seeing something else, something far away. "When I came back from the war, I wasn't much use to your mother. In fact, I said to her, 'I'm not much use to you, am I?' And you know what she said to me? She said 'No, you're not. I'm giving you three months.'"

Sid had heard this story before. His mother truly had given their father a deadline—some time to sort himself out. That deadline was well past.

"They invalided me out of the army, right at the end of the war. When I was better, they gave me a medical. Said I was fit, and I could take any job I liked."

Sid knew this too, although his father had never told him about it. It was knowledge he had gleaned from overhearing conversations between his parents and from Beryl's whispered information. Beryl always knew what was going on.

Dad went on. "So I said, 'Great, I've got a job waiting for me back in the army, as a sergeant.' Then the doctor says, 'Oh no, you're not fit enough for that!' And he gave me a pension. A pension! You can't live on it! And if you try and get a bit of work, under the table, all the work you can get is hoeing swedes and turnips. And people glare at you because you're working on a pension."

This was true. People thought badly of Dad if he worked, saying other men needed the work, men without pensions.

"Don't you want to help the family, Sidney?" Dad had an unfair way of putting things.

"Yes," said Sid.

"Well then, you'll be looking for a job. Not more education. Not spending time at the racetrack. And not some pipe-dream about being a jockey. Think about your brothers and sisters."

Sid thought about them. Especially Beryl.

Beryl's sixteen, and still at school. She'll be a teacher one day. Not that I begrudge her the opportunity.

"I just want a chance to follow my dream, too," he muttered unconsciously.

"What was that you said?" Dad raised his voice.

"Nothing, Dad."

"Follow your dream?" Dad had heard, all right. "Follow your dream? What is this? La-la-land?"

Dad stood up, shoving the table. The unlit cigarette rolled to the very edge and teetered there. Sid stared at it, watching it wobble. Dad began to pace. In the tiny kitchen, he seemed like a giant. The twins froze, their spoons dripping porridge.

"This is meant to be a land fit for heroes to come back to. Hah! They said that after the last war, and now they've said it again. And it still means nothing! There's nothing to come home to, but a lot of hungry mouths. And some good mates you'll never see again."

"Dad, I..."

"Don't open your mouth until you're told to," yelled Dad.

"Arthur?" It was Mum, tiny next to her husband. "Arthur, the boy needs to strain the milk. And have his breakfast."

"Oh yes, the boy needs to have his breakfast!" Dad was shouting now. "Poor wee lad, he needs to eat! Well, I hope he knows where the money's coming from to pay for the porridge. Because I know it went on the slate."

"I did ask Mr Cunningham if I could pay him later, yes." Mum's voice was steady.

"We don't need his charity," said Dad.

"It's not charity, Arthur. He knows we'll pay. The Cunninghams have known our family for years. They can trust us to pay them."

"Well, I've had enough of it," said Dad. "No more. If we can't pay, we won't eat."

"And what about if we can't pay, we don't drink?" Mum's shoulders went back, her chin went up. "What about you shouting the bar? Eh? I know where our money went to. 'Drinks for everyone! I'm shouting the bar!'" Mum's face was flushed. "You didn't think about your family then, did you? And your mate Jack, and all that lot down the pub, they won't say no to a free drink. They won't remind you you've got a wife and five children."

Sid backed away to stand by his brothers. They had put their spoons down and were watching, open-mouthed.

Mum seemed to grow bigger before their eyes. "I stick up for you all the time, Arthur Everett. I never let you down. But you let our family down every week." She glared up at her husband. He didn't answer, so she kept going. "The other day, Angie Dawson at the butcher's told me you were a fool to have gone off to the war. That you didn't have to volunteer, a man with five children. I told her she was right. I said, 'Yes, he was a fool, Angie. To go off risking his life for ungrateful people like you!'" Mum's voice shook. "I stick up for you all the time, Arthur Everett. It's time you started doing the same for us."

Dad stared at her. His shoulders drooped. Suddenly, he didn't seem such a tall man. He picked up his hat and stumbled out of the kitchen, bumping Beryl aside as he went.

There was a long silence, then Beryl spoke. "Mum. I've got something to tell you."

"Yes, Beryl?"

"I'm getting a job."

"What do you mean?" said Mum.

Beryl lifted her chin. "I've got a job interview in town. At Miller's Drapery."

"Beryl, you can't!" said Mum. "You haven't finished school. You're going to be a teacher!"

"It's all right, Mum." Beryl was calm. "It's not that important. I don't mind a shop job."

"No, Beryl."

"I've decided, Mum. The interview's this weekend. On Saturday morning." She turned to Sid. "Can you take me in on Hugh? I don't want to get my shoes muddy, walking." She wheeled around and strode out of the kitchen.

Sid looked at Mum. Then he raced after his sister.

Chapter Six

Knocked Back

"Beryl! Wait!" Sid had to run. His sister was already on the track leading up the hill. "Beryl. Hang on a minute. Let me talk to you."

Beryl stopped. She didn't turn around. When Sid caught up with her, he saw her eyes were full of tears.

"Beryl, you can't do it!" Sid was breathing hard.

"Keep out of it, Sid. I've made up my mind," she said. "I've got an interview and everything."

Sid searched her face, wondering what to say. "Beryl, you can't just throw away your future. And you'll *hate* a shop job. You'll be bored in five minutes."

"How do you know?" snapped Beryl. "You don't know everything about me, Sid Everett."

Sid blinked. The furious words pounding through his head as he ran seemed to have left him. He tried to recapture them. "What about teaching? What about your dream?"

"It's not everything, Sid." Her lips quivered.

"And what about going away to Christchurch or Auckland? Like you told Mr Cowley." Sid frowned. "Why Christchurch or Auckland, anyway?"

"Because of Ruby."

"Ruby?" he asked.

"Because then she can to go to Deaf School," said Beryl. "There's Sumner, the deaf school in Christchurch, or there's a new one in Auckland."

"Oh. I didn't think," said Sid.

"That's all right, nobody expected you to. Mum talked to me about it. Before the war, all the deaf kids went to Sumner. But during the war, they thought the ferry crossing was too dangerous, so they opened a new school in Auckland." She shrugged. "Any deaf school is a long way from here. But if I was at Training College, nearby..."

"Oh, I see."

"Yeah. But I can't do anything about that now," she said.

"Why not? It's perfect."

Beryl stared past him, her eyes unseeing. "I don't think it's true, what they tell you."

"What?" said Sid.

"That you can be anything you want when you grow up. It's a lie. It's just not always possible." She took a deep breath. "We have to face it. There are dreams and there's real life, and they're not the same. We just have to accept it."

Sid stared. "What the...?" He clenched his fists, then opened his hands, stretching his fingers as wide as they would go. "What kind of talk is that? How can you even say that? You mustn't give up!"

Beryl turned and looked at him. "I'm not giving up, Sid. It's not giving up. It's just facing reality. We need money. I can get a job. That's what I'm doing."

"Beryl!"

"Sid." Beryl's voice was gentle. "Sid, most girls get married anyway. I probably will too. Within a few years. I know it seems crazy now, but in a few years' time it won't matter what I did, where I worked. I'll be cooking and cleaning and looking after children. That's reality. That's real life. And Sid?"

"What?"

"I am happy, knowing that I'm helping Mum."

Sid frowned, baffled and still angry. His heart pounded and his own breath was loud in his ears. He thought of something else. "Well, I don't agree. Becoming a teacher is much more important than helping Mum with money. She can manage. Or I can help her. Or maybe Dad..." He paused. "And what about Ruby? Going to Deaf School? You just told me that when you're at Training College, you can be near her. If you leave school and get a stupid job, what about that?

"Don't be upset, Sid." Beryl gave him a crooked smile. "Mum just won't let her go, that's all. Not until she's absolutely sure she'll be all right. Ruby's old enough to be at school already, but Mum hasn't allowed it. She needs to feel sure she's safe, at Deaf School." She punched him on the arm. "I'll be all right. Just have Hugh all ready for me, Saturday morning. First thing."

After a long moment, Sid sighed. "All right. If that's what you want." He rubbed his jaw. It was aching from the way he'd been clenching his teeth. "But I think you're making a big mistake. I'm going to try something. I'll go and see Mr Thorndon. See if he'll take me on."

***

The morning sun between the trees stretched long shadows across the Thorndon's driveway, making the sunlight flicker across his eyes as he walked. He breathed in the fresh, damp smell of ferns and earth. The din of cicadas singing high in the overhead branches made him almost dizzy. As he approached the Thorndon residence, his heart began hammering in his chest.

Sid realised it wasn't just the walk that made him breathe harder, or his awkward mission. He was approaching Sarah's house. He hoped he wouldn't run into her. He needed to focus on what he was going to say to her father.

Should he be doing this? Mr Thorndon had said next year, sort of. But remembering Beryl's face, he was determined to ask right now. If he could get some sort of work, perhaps he could stop his sister from throwing away her future. Any sort of work would do. Later, he would worry about his own dream.

As he neared the house, the front door opened and two men came out onto the wide veranda. One of them was talking, but then his voice stopped. They had spotted him. It was too late to turn back now. He saw that one was Mr Thorndon. The other looked like the man he had bumped into at the races, the one who had called him a young jockey. He felt their eyes on him as he approached.

"Good morning, young man."

"Good morning, Mr Thorndon," said Sid.

The other man raised his eyebrows. "Oh! It's the young fellow from the races. The one who wasn't actually a jockey."

Mr Thorndon gave a small smile. "Dad, this is Sidney Everett, our neighbour. Sidney, this is my father, Major Thorndon. He's out from the old country for a visit."

So that's who he was. Sarah's grandfather. Sid nodded in the older man's direction. "Good morning, sir."

Mr Thorndon became business-like. "What can I do for you, Master Everett?"

"Well, Mr Thorndon, I know you said you're not hiring apprentices now..."

"That's right."

"Well, I was wondering...." Sid struggled to get a grip on his thoughts. "Something's come up, in our family. I can't really explain. I would like to apply for a job, sir. Any sort of job. Anything at all. I can do all kinds of farm work. I can groom and feed your horses. I'll wash your car or do your garden. Anything."

"Sorry, Sidney, I don't have anything at the moment." Mr Thorndon was matter-of-fact. "There's nothing available right now. I recently took on a man to help with the stables. He's got a lot of experience with horses. But I don't need anyone else."

Sid felt his face flush. What had he been thinking? Of course, there wasn't any work.

Mr Thorndon's face softened. "Sidney, we get men coming here almost every week, asking for a job. It's not as bad as it was before the war, but there are still a lot of men out there looking for work." He paused. "And aren't you still at school?"

"Yes," said Sid.

"Then my advice to you is to stay at school and get the best education that you can."

"Yes, sir. That's what Mr Cowley says." So that was it, then. No point in lingering, especially when his face felt like it was going as red as a beetroot. He nodded to the two men. "Good day."

He turned and walked away, sensing their eyes on his back. He longed to run, but forced himself to walk steadily, boots crunching on the gravel, towards the shelter of the tree-lined driveway. Tears pricked his eyes, and he blinked hard, determined not to cry. There had to be another way to help Beryl.

As Sid reached the driveway and the shade of the trees, he heard the clip clop of hooves somewhere ahead. Beyond the curve of the driveway, a rider was approaching. He took a deep breath, squared his shoulders, and kept walking. Around the bend he had a view down the long avenue of trees. Sarah was on horseback, coming towards him. He stopped and waited.

"Good morning, Sid!" She halted her horse as she reached him.

"Hello, Sarah."

"Fancy seeing you here! Have you been talking to my dad?"

"Um, yes," said Sid. That was correct, more or less.

Sarah smiled down at him. "It's a lovely morning, isn't it? I love to go out for a ride when it's like this."

Sid felt his troubles disappear. He reached out a hand and stroked the horse's soft nose. "Yes, it's a beautiful morning for a ride."

"This is my new pony, Talley. That's short for Talisman. You know - for good luck. Isn't she lovely?"

"She's beautiful." Sid grinned up at Sarah. "She suits you."

Sarah laughed. "Dad spoils me." She looked at Sid and raised an eyebrow. "What were you talking to him about? You weren't asking for a job, were you?"

"Yes, actually," said Sid.

"I suppose he turned you down?" she asked.

"Yup," said Sid.

Sarah sighed. "He gets people asking for work all the time. He has to say no." She pulled a face. "I'm glad it's not me who has to stand there saying 'no, sorry.' But Sid!" Her eyes widened. "Why are you looking for work? You can't leave school now. You haven't finished the year."

"I've done enough school, Sarah. Enough for me, anyway. I'm almost fifteen, and nobody will care if I leave early. Except maybe old Cowley. I need to earn some money."

"There'll be hardly anybody left! I'll have to put up with that horrid Roger."

Horrid Roger, eh? Sid hid a satisfied smile. "Well, if I don't get a job, I guess I'll carry on at school. But..."

"Yes?"

"My sister..." Sid's voice trailed off.

"Beryl?" asked Sarah.

"Yes," said Sid. "She's leaving school to get a job in a shop—she thinks she has to help the family. That means she's giving up on being a teacher. And I don't think she should."

Sarah frowned. "You're right!"

"So, I thought, perhaps if I got a job, I could help the family instead of her. And Beryl could stay on at school. I'm taking her for an interview on Saturday morning, in town. She's pretty determined."

"I wish I could help," said Sarah.

He smiled. "Not to worry. Something will turn up." He wished he felt as hopeful as his words sounded. "I'd better get back home."

"All right, Sid. Tell her I said good luck."

"I will. Bye, Sarah."

He stepped aside. Sarah tapped her heels against her horse's sides and rode on.

Sid strolled the rest of the driveway with a smile on his face. The 'no' from Mr Thorndon no longer stung. To be honest, what had he expected, anyway? Now he needed to forget about it. He would go and see Hugh. Hugh was always comforting. He'd spend some time with him and give him a good brush. Get him ready for the trip to town in the weekend.

***

Approaching the house, Sid heard raised voices. Mum sounded upset. What now? He pushed the door open. "Mum? I'm back."

In the kitchen, Dad was sitting at the table. Mum was by the fireplace, holding a letter.

"Oh, Sid." She waved the letter at him. "I've been putting off opening this. I've had it hidden behind the things on the mantelpiece. But today, I dared to open it. And we've been... talking about it."

"What's it about?" asked Sid.

She handed him the envelope. "It's nothing I didn't know already. I suppose I hoped it might go away if I ignored it."

Sid read aloud.

"Dear Mrs Everett. Following on from our previous corre-spondence, (our letter dated the 26th of May 1946) and having received no response from you, we advise again that you are obliged, under the Education Act, to ensure that your daughter Ruby Grace Everett receives a full education from the age of six years.

Your failure to comply with this legal requirement can result in action from the Crown. In consideration of this, and with concern for your daughter's welfare and future, we wish to arrange a meeting with you to discuss, face to face, the options that are available to you to provide an education for your deaf child.

Yours faithfully, J R Baldwin."

Sid looked up. "It makes you sound like a criminal!"

Mum laughed. "That's what your father said."

Dad stood up. "She has to go, Mary."

"She won't manage at school," said Mum. "The boys can't look after her. None of them are in the junior class. She'd learn nothing, and she'd be miserable. And she's not going away to Deaf School, living in a strange town, with strangers. Who's going to look after her?"

"Other people send their children," said Dad.

"I'm not 'other people'. I'm me, and I'm going to protect my daughter. She's deaf, for goodness' sake. She needs looking after."

"All the other ones are deaf, too," said Dad. "That's what these schools are for." His voice softened. "Mary, she's going to need some education. Learn to talk, if she can. She's got to grow up and live in the world."

Mum sighed. "I know. It's just...she's so little, Arthur!"

"And here we go again. Around the mulberry bush." Dad brushed past Sid and went outside, leaving the door open.

Mum gazed after him. "Oh, Sid. I feel as though I'll have to get a gun and fight them off. My Ruby!"

"It's not that bad, Mum." Sid grinned. "I'd like to see you with a gun, fighting off the Department of Education." He put the letter on the mantelpiece. In plain sight, not hidden. "But Mum, something does have to happen for Ruby. Beryl had a good plan, but..." He shook his head, shaking out the jumble of thoughts. "Write back to them. Go to the meeting. Find out as much as you can."

"You're right, Sid. That's exactly what your father said. I just..." She threw up her hands. "Yes, I'll write to them. And go to the meeting." She gave Sid a sudden, fierce hug. "Oh Sid. Just as well I've got you and Beryl. It's one thing after another around here."

"That's for sure." Sid hesitated. "Mum? I don't think Beryl's going to change her mind about the job. I tried to talk to her."

Mum sighed. "I can't budge her, either. She's absolutely determined. She wants to help."

"We all want to help," said Sid.

"Yes, I know you do, love, and you help me enormously. All the time."

Sid squirmed, unused to praise. "I'll um, go and give Hugh a brush. Get him shining. For Saturday."

"Saturday?" asked Mum.

"Beryl's interview."

"Oh. Yes." Mum's eyes held Sid's for a time before turning away. "The interview."

Chapter Seven

Holding The Horse

"Oooh, I'm stiff!" Beryl hobbled around on the grass, smoothing her dress.

"Well, you insisted on riding!" Sid stroked Hugh's nose and led him over to a wooden fence.

"Are you coming with me," asked Beryl, "or are you going to wait here with Hugh?"

"I'm coming with you." Sid tied Hugh to the railing in front of the picnic area.

Beryl bent down and rubbed her shoes with her hand, then stood up straight. "How do I look?"

"Fine," said Sid.

"Thanks." She grinned. "Like a shop lady?"

"No. Like a schoolgirl."

"Unh!" Beryl pulled a face. "Well, too bad! Come on, Sid. Let's go."

The low, early morning sun slanted in under the shop awnings on the sunny side of the street. Voices sounded distantly in the still air, and a car engine roared into life somewhere nearby. The shops were all closed. Sparrows dust-bathed among the sandy pebbles on either side of the sealed road.

Sid grinned. "Looks like the Wild West. A deserted street, just before the Lone Ranger rides into town..."

"Sid!" Beryl hissed. She nodded towards the draper's shop. "She's in there already." She hesitated. "Don't come with me. This won't take long. You can wait for me here."

"I'll go for a walk," said Sid. "See you soon."

Sid strolled along the empty main street. Although all the shops were closed, the hotel was open. Somebody was sweeping the steps, and sash windows rattled up, ready for the day. Sid wandered over, smelling the musty beer and cigarette smell that drifted out into the sunlight.

In the distance, a horse and rider appeared, moving slowly up the street. Sid smiled to himself. It really did look like something from the Lone Ranger. As the rider approached, he recognised old Captain Findlay, retired World War One army captain. A man who loved horses. Just about the only person around who still rode a horse to town.

"Good morning, young fellow!" The captain stopped his horse outside the hotel. "Fine morning."

"Yes, sir," said Sid.

The captain dismounted. "Hold my horse for me, will you, just for a minute? Got to see a man about a dog."

"Sure." Sid took the reins and watched as the captain marched into the hotel. He turned to the horse. "Fine fellow, aren't you?" He stroked the bay's glossy neck, admiring the shine on his coat and the polish on the captain's saddle.

A voice shouted, "Hey, Everett!"

Sid turned to observe Roger Dyson, smartly dressed, coming around the corner. The last person he wanted to meet. "Morning, Dyson."

"Stole a horse?" said Roger.

"What?" said Sid.

"That doesn't look like your horse," Roger sneered.

Sid kept his voice steady. "This is Captain Findlay's horse, Dyson."

"Aah!" Roger reached out a hand, but the horse lifted his head and backed away.

"He doesn't like you," said Sid. He stroked the horse's neck, steadying him.

"All horses like me. He's just retarded." Roger scowled and walked away. "Nasty animal."

Sid watched with narrowed eyes as Roger disappeared into an alleyway. He continued to stroke the horse, talking to him soothingly. The captain was taking a while.

I wonder how Beryl's interview's going?

The ping of something hitting the pavement interrupted his thoughts. The horse started. Another ping, and the horse began prancing and tossing his head. Sid felt something hit him on the cheek. A small stone. Someone was flicking stones!

"Easy, boy. Easy!" Sid walked the gelding around in a circle, talking to him, calming him down. Another stone flicked, and Sid saw it hit the horse on the rump. As the horse danced sideways, Sid ran with him, still holding the rein, talking to him all the time. "Easy, boy! That's it. Good boy."

"Hey, you there!" It was the captain, on the steps of the hotel. "You! Boy!" Sid froze, but the Captain wasn't looking at him. He was looking at another boy, on the upstairs balcony of the hotel. Roger Dyson.

"Young fool! Wait until I talk to your father!" The captain shook his fist. "I know who you are. Young idiot! Upsetting my horse. Endangering people. Your father's going to hear about this!" The captain stormed across to where Sid stood, holding his horse.

"You did a splendid job there, lad! I saw the whole thing—couldn't believe my eyes!" Captain Findlay took the reins from Sid. "What's the matter with that boy? I know his father well. I shall certainly be having words with him!"

Sid glanced away, then looked back at the Captain. "He was trying to bother me, sir, rather than your horse."

"Trying to bother you, eh?" said the Captain. "And why should he do that?"

Sid shuffled uncomfortably. "Don't know, sir."

"I'll tell you why. He's a fool and a bully, that's why," said the Captain, stroking his horse. "Unbelievable! Well, I sent him away with a flea in his ear!" Calming down, the captain's manner changed. "Actually, I don't think he's a very happy boy. From a wealthy home. Plenty of money and all that, but money isn't everything. Not by a long chalk. They put a lot of pressure on him. He's their only child. Got to make them proud." He shook his head. "They're ruining him."

Captain Findlay studied Sid more closely. "You're good with a horse. You're Arthur Everett's boy, aren't you?"

"Yes, sir. Sid." Feeling awkward, Sid reached out a hand to the horse's soft muzzle.

"Sid. Yes." The captain nodded, still reassuringly stroking his horse. "Your father did himself proud in the war. Not coping too well now, though. Or so I hear."

"No, sir. Not too well," said Sid.

"Damn shame!" The captain peered at Sid again. "Like horses, don't you?"

"Yes sir." Sid suddenly had a wild hope. "You don't want somebody to work for you, do you? With your horses?"

"Hmmm," said the Captain. "No."

"Oh," said Sid.

"But..." The Captain pondered. "I mean, I don't need to employ anyone."

"Yes?" said Sid.

"But maybe I could use someone part time. Would you be interested in exercising my horses?"

"Come over and ride them?" asked Sid.

"Yes. Ride them around. Valuable experience for you. And it will make my lazy lot do a bit of work. You could do some mucking out, too."

"Yes, sir, I'd love to." Sid paused. "I would have to ask my dad, though."

"Of course, of course." Captain Findlay mounted his horse. "I'll be off. Good day to you, young Everett." He nodded. "I'll look forward to hearing from you."

Sid watched the captain ride away, then turned and walked back towards the draper's shop. No sign of Roger, anywhere. His heart leapt and his steps quickened, thinking about what he had been offered. How things could change in a moment!

"Hey, Sid!" Beryl bounced over to him. "I got the job!"

"Good for you, Beryl!" Sid tried to smile.

"What's up?" Beryl eyed him, her head on one side.

"I tried," said Sid. "With Mr Thorndon."

"I know you did," said Beryl. "But it's all right." She looked at him again. "There's something else, isn't there?"

"I just had an interesting meeting," said Sid.

"Yeah? Tell me as we walk back to Hugh."

Together, they strolled towards the park.

"Well," said Sid. "I was holding Captain Findlay's horse in front of the pub." He glanced at Beryl, walking beside him. "Roger Dyson came along and started flicking stones at him. At the horse, I mean, not the captain."

"Really!" said Beryl. "That Roger Dyson is such a pain!"

"Yeah, I'll say!" said Sid. "He came and talked to me, at first, being all superior as usual. Then he went off. He must have sneaked into the hotel and gone up onto the balcony. The horse was jumping around, and I was trying to hold on to him. He's a big horse! I tried to calm him down, and the captain came out and saw what was happening. He gave Dyson a real telling off."

"You're good with horses, Sid," said Beryl.

"That's what the captain said. And Beryl—guess what? He wants me to go to his place and exercise his horses!"

"Is that good?" asked Beryl.

"It's fantastic! It's actually paid work! Part time. I can have a go at riding a decent horse, do some fast riding, try some jumps. It'll be like jockey training!"

"You'll have to ask Mum and Dad."

"Yeah." Sid's face darkened. "But surely they'll say yes. What problem could they have with it?"

Beryl didn't reply.

As they reached the picnic area, Sid remembered why they had come to town.

"So, tell me about the interview. What did she say?"

Beryl shrugged. "She was nice. Her name's Mrs Archibald. I think she'd already decided that she wanted me. She said I was a bright girl."

"You are," said Sid.

"She asked me why I was leaving school now, and not waiting until the end of the year."

"What did you say?"

"I said we needed the money at home," said Beryl. "And she said she understood."

Sid frowned. "Does she know you're practically top of the school? Does she realise you were going to be a teacher?"

"I think she knows more than I thought, Sid. More than she let on. Because she started telling me all about how she gave up school when she was only twelve years old to help her family."

"Twelve? Was that even legal?"

"Her mother had just had twins, and then she died. So she left school at twelve, to look after newborn twins and three other children."

"Oh," said Sid.

"Yeah, 'Oh'," said Beryl. "It sort of puts things into perspective, doesn't it? Hearing how things used to be. She said sometimes you have to make sacrifices, but you never regret doing the right thing."

"I suppose so. If it is actually the right thing," said Sid.

"Well, let's say it is. I feel a lot better now, anyway. I think I'll enjoy working for her."

"That's good." Sid smiled at his sister. "Let's get you home." He helped Beryl up onto Hugh's back and untied the lead reins. "Time to make your legs all stiff again."

Leading Hugh, Sid headed out along the road home. Surely Mum and Dad wouldn't object to him exercising the Captain's horses? It was actually paid work. But he had a sinking feeling that they wouldn't perceive it as the great opportunity he thought it was.

Chapter Eight

Another Way

Sid carried the heavy milk bucket into the gloom of the scullery and lifted it up onto the bench, then went across to the house for hot water. The morning sun was warm on his back, and Mum's geraniums by the door glowed bright red. Their leaves gave off their distinct, pungent smell as he brushed past them.

Mum was cooking porridge. "It's nearly ready, Sid," she said.

"I won't be long, Mum," said Sid. He grabbed the kettle from the coal range.

As he went back to the scullery, he heard Dad in the shed, whistling. Whistling was a good sign. Dad must be in a cheerful mood. Perhaps this morning he would dare to ask about exercising Captain Findlay's horses.

Sid scalded the cloth, strained the milk, and hurried to the house for breakfast.

The family, all except Dad, was sitting at the breakfast table. As he reached for the milk, he caught Ruby's eye and rubbed his tummy. "Good porridge, Ruby?"

Ruby nodded, grinning.

Dad's footsteps sounded on the back porch. Sid noticed everyone sat up straighter. "Morning, family." Dad took his place at the head of the table and made a flourish of adding milk and sugar to his porridge. "Yum!"

Sid knew his father didn't enjoy porridge. He would rather eat bacon and eggs on a Sunday morning, but porridge was what they could afford, so everyone had to like it. He waited until his dad had eaten a few mouthfuls and then spoke up.

"Dad?"

"Yes, son?" said Dad.

"I met Captain Findlay in town the other day."

"Findlay? The old fella?"

"The retired army captain. From the first war."

"I know who he is," snapped Dad.

Sid steeled himself. "Well, Dad, I was wondering... He asked me if I'd like to come and exercise his horses for him."

"What do you mean, exercise them?" Dad reached for more milk.

"Well, you know, ride them. Make them do stuff. Go round the round pen, jump over jumps, get them behaving them-selves..."

Dad interrupted him. "No, you can't."

"Why not?" Sid regretted the words as soon as they were out of his mouth.

Dad put down his spoon and gave Sid a hard look. "How far away does he live, Sidney?"

"Quite far," said Sid.

"Quite far." Dad's voice got louder. "Yes, quite far. On the other side of town, actually. And then a bit further. How long would it take you to get there?"

"On Hugh? Not long," said Sid.

"So after school, you'd come home and do your homework, and your jobs. Then you'd get on Hugh and ride over to Findlay's place. And that would take you 'not long'. Then you'd exercise his horses. For how long? An hour? Two hours?" Dad waited for an answer.

"I don't know," said Sid.

"You don't know," said Dad. "So, say you exercise his horses for an hour or two. Then you get on Hugh and ride back here again. What time is it when you get back?"

Sid's heart had already sunk down into his boots. He answered in a low voice, "Quite late, I suppose."

"You're darn right, it would be quite late." Dad stared around at the family. Everyone sat frozen in their seats. He looked back at Sid. "Nope, and that means no."

Sid knew he should leave it at that, but he tried again. "Dad, he asked me because he needs help with his horses. And I need somewhere where I can ride a horse that's got a bit more spark than Hugh has. And he'll pay me It's paid work."

Dad was listening, so Sid carried on. "I could go straight from school. That would be quicker. I could come back here and do my homework later." Sid glanced at Mum. She was standing by the kitchen sink. She inclined her head slightly. That meant she thought it would work. He thought of something else. "And Dad, he said you did yourself proud in the war."

"Did he? Did he indeed?" Dad got that far-away expression for a minute, then he snapped back to the family and Sid. "Nope. My answer's still no. Your mother needs you. The family needs you. In the winter, it'd be dark before you even got to Findlay's."

"But Dad!" For a minute, Sid has been almost certain that Dad would agree.

Dad was suddenly angry. "Don't you 'but Dad' me! Don't you answer back! I'll tell you what you can do since you've got so much spare time and you want to earn some money." His voice was getting louder. "Since you've got so much spare time after school, you can work with me."

"Work?" said Sid.

"Yes, work! Don't like the sound of it? Well, get used to it. It's what life's full of!"

Sid sat and waited, not sure where Dad was going.

"Sidney?" said Dad.

"Yes, Dad?"

"After school tomorrow, you can head out to McKenzie's farm. Go to the house. Tell them you're my son and you want to start work with me."

Sid was speechless.

"Did you hear me, son?"

"Yes, Dad," said Sid.

"Tomorrow after school," said Dad. "Don't forget. They'll send you out to where I'm hoeing turnips." Dad pushed his chair back. "All right. Back to the shed." He walked out of the kitchen.

"Sid!" Beryl was looking at him, stricken. "Maybe he'll forget?"

"Yeah, and maybe he won't. I'll have to go." Sid felt bitterness rising up inside. "He's been wanting this for a long time. All he wants is to get me working. Earning money."

"That'll do, Sidney Everett!" Mum cut him short. "You're not to speak about your father like that. It's disrespectful. It won't hurt you to go after school and earn some money."

Sid knew Mum felt sorry for him, but she would always stay loyal to Dad. He shoved his chair back. "Yeah, thanks, Mum!" He stomped out of the kitchen, only realising as he reached the back porch that he had acted just like his father.

He headed round to the back of the barn, needing somewhere to be alone. Perhaps he should just go ahead and pack a few things and leave home.

Yeah, that was it. Just leave. Get out of here.

He kicked the wall of the barn.

But even as he thought it, he knew he couldn't leave Mum. Couldn't leave Ruby and the twins. Not until things were better. He leaned his back against the sun-baked wooden wall, rough with flaking paint, and closed his eyes, trying not to think about anything. Distantly, he heard voices calling him.

The twins. I don't want to talk to them. Not to anyone. Maybe they wouldn't try the barn.

He opened the door and slipped inside.

The barn was dusty and dim and smelled of hay and warm wood. Sid climbed to the loft, the ladder creaking under his bare feet. He hadn't been up here since he'd hidden his newspaper cuttings. Sudden anxiety clutched at his heart, and he hurried to the dark corner where he'd stashed his collection under some planks of wood. He lifted the boards and pulled out a big, round tin, prised the lid open, and there they were. He let out a long breath he hadn't realised he'd been holding. They were dry, clean, and safe. He had missed seeing them on his wall, but he couldn't risk losing them. And he hadn't lost his determination. He was more determined than ever.

With a twinge of sadness, he replaced the lid and hid the tin back under the pile of wood. Then he crossed the dusty wooden floor of the loft and peered out of the single small window. It wasn't actually a window, merely an opening where a hook used to hang for hauling bales of hay. He gazed around. From up here, the neat paddocks of the Thorndon property next door were clearly visible. Several horses were grazing, only a paddock away. From the ground, a dense, prickly row of tōtara trees always hid them from sight, but up here he had a perfect view of them. A gate in their paddock led out onto the unsealed road that wound its way to the sea.

What if...?
Ideas pounded through his mind.
What if I could ride one of Mr Thorndon's horses? I'm sure he'd let me. Just around the paddock. Maybe even down the lane. Or up the hill. They've got miles of land. I'm sure he'd say yes!
His mind was racing.

Maybe along the beach? Would he let me? Perhaps not. Best not to mention it. But what if he said yes? The beach would be perfect.

He heard his brothers' voices outside, and peered down. The twins were directly below, looking for him.

"Hey boys!"

They looked up. "Oh, there you are," said Bruce.

"I've got an idea," said Sid. "Wait, I'll come down." He scrambled down the ladder.

The twins were waiting at the bottom. "What were you doing up there?"

"Nothing. Do you want to hear my idea?"

"What is it?" asked Bill.

"Well, you know I want to be a jockey?"

"Yes," they said.

"So, I need a fast horse. To practise on. To get good at riding."

The twins stared at him.

Sid led them outside. "There are lots of horses next door. Mr Thorndon's horses. I was looking at them from the loft. And I think Mr Thorndon would let me ride one. He knows me. He knows I can ride."

Bill frowned. "You'd have to ask."

"Of course I would ask," said Sid. "I wouldn't just take one. Those horses are worth a fortune."

"Really?" asked Bruce.

"Well, yes, some of them are very valuable," said Sid. "But there must be at least one I could ride." He grinned at them. "Come with me. We'll go through the fence and have a look at them."

***

Tōtara leaves prickled against Sid's arms and face as he pushed through into the paddock next door. Bill and Bruce followed close behind.

"It's really nice here!" Bill gazed around. The paddock was like a little park, with smooth, even grass. It had a few enormous shade trees and a stream running through.

Bruce whistled. "A bit different to our place!"

Sid gazed around, breathing in the peace of the paddock. Even the sun seemed warmer here.

"Sid! What about this one?" Bruce was being followed by a small pony. "It's really friendly."

"That's Sarah's horse, Talley," said Sid. "I wouldn't ask to ride her." He held out his hand, and she nuzzled it. "She's too small, anyway." He gazed around. "It would make sense to find a horse about the same size as Hugh, so I can use his saddle and bridle."

"That's a nice one." Bill pointed to a dark bay on the far side of the paddock. "Looks like Hugh. Younger though, I think."

"Yeah," said Sid. He approached the horse. It moved away. Sid stopped, then deliberately turned his back. Slowly, the horse's curiosity overcame its caution, and Sid felt its breath on the back of his neck.

"You're a fine fellow!" Sid stroked the soft nose, noticing a few little dark marks where some hair was missing. The whiskers on the horse's chin brushed against his cheek. "Aren't you?" The horse dipped his head.

Bill laughed. "He's saying 'yes.'"

"Yeah, I think so." Sid smoothed back the mane and stroked the horse's powerful neck. He whispered, "You look like a goer. Want to go riding with me?" The horse shook his head and snorted.

"You want to ride him?" Bruce was watching, his head on one side.

"Yes!" Sid was suddenly sure that this was the horse, that this was his ticket to success. He frowned at his brothers. "You can't tell anyone."

"Why not?" asked Bill.

"Because Dad wouldn't like it," said Sid.

"All right." The boys nodded.

"Good," said Sid.

"Can we come with you when you ask Mr Thorndon?" said Bruce.

"No, I'll ride over on Hugh." Sid's heart was pounding. He couldn't wait to get started. "Come on, boys, let's go back home. Oh, hang on for a minute. I just want to look at something…" He walked over and checked the gate. "No padlock. Just a hook. Easy."

Back at the barn, Sid faced his brothers. "I'm swearing you to secrecy. Understand? Because Dad would get mad."

"Yeah, we understand. When are you going to Mr Thorndon's?"

"I'll go now." He grinned at their excited faces. "If anyone's looking for me, you don't know where I am."

Chapter Nine

View From The Hill

Sid rode Hugh over to the Thorndon's. Their driveway seemed quite different on horseback. Cool, inviting, and not very long. He rode up to the house and wondered what to do next.

"Sidney Everett. What can I do for you?" Mr Thorndon appeared from around the corner, squinting in the sun.

"Hello, Mr Thorndon," said Sid. "I wanted to ask you something."

"Ask away, Sidney. Happy to help, if I can."

"Well, you know I want to be a jockey. I mean, one day."

"Yes." Mr Thorndon moved into the shade, took off his hat, and wiped his forehead with his sleeve.

"I was wondering," said Sid. "You have a lot of nice horses. I've got Hugh, but he's not very fast..."

"Hugh? Is this him? Hello, Hugh." Mr Thorndon moved forward to stroke Hugh's nose, and ran practiced hands down his chest and legs. "Fine boy. Getting on now, I suppose?"

"Yes." Sid's muscles were tense. He took a deep breath and made himself relax. "Would you have a horse, do you think, that I could ride, to practise on? Not one of your very valuable ones, of course. Just one that's sort of quite fast, but not so valuable." He knew he was talking too fast, and he could feel himself going red in the face.

Mr Thorndon smiled. "I think I understand what you mean."

Sid felt a weight lift off his shoulders.

"Come with me, Sidney," said Mr Thorndon. "You can lead Hugh around the back and I'll show you where you can tie him up for a bit."

Sid followed Mr Thorndon to a small paddock where horses were grazing. He looked up and over the trees and saw his family's barn. He knew exactly where he was.

"There's one here," Mr Thorndon said, gazing around, "that I think would be just right for you. Silver." He whistled, and Sid turned to see a dark bay horse approaching.

"Silver? This one?" he asked.

"That's right," said Mr Thorndon. "Silver. But not by colour." He smiled. "Not like the Lone Ranger's horse."

"No," said Sid.

"His name's Silver Lining. Silver for short. I've had him for a while. I'm never going to sell him. He's not a winner, but I'm quite attached to him. He's a special boy."

"Hello, Silver." Sid stroked the soft nose, a smile spreading over his face. It was the same horse that had followed him when he'd been here with his brothers. Everything seemed to be falling into place.

Mr Thorndon was still talking. "Excellent bloodlines. By Sir Wilton, that's the stallion, out of Black Widow. She was a lovely mare. Stunners, both of them. Produced some top horses. But poor old Silver, he took a tumble in an early race. Never got his edge back. He lost that drive to win." Mr Thorndon stroked the horse's dark neck. "He's a lovely boy. He used to go like the wind, but he was a bit shy of the fight."

He sighed. "We've had some terrific rides." He put his nose to Silver's nose. "Eh, boy?"

"Are you sure?" asked Sid. "I mean, are you sure about me riding him?" His stomach lurched with sudden anxiety. This horse obviously meant a lot to Mr Thorndon.

"Absolutely," said Mr Thorndon. "You're a good rider. And a sensible boy. You can go around the next paddock and along the race, and along the lane too, if you want. And you can always go up the hill." He waved his arm at the high, grassy hills behind the paddocks. "You can go for miles up there. See for miles, too."

"Thank you very much, Mr Thorndon."

"That's alright, Sid. Want to ride him now?"

"Yes, please!"

Mr Thorndon found some riding gear and watched as Sid saddled up. "Good boy. You know what you're doing. Let's see you, then."

Feeling awkward, Sid mounted and stroked Silver's neck, talking to him softly. He gathered the reins and pressed his heels against Silver's flanks, starting off at a walk around the paddock before moving into a trot. Mr Thorndon studied him for a few minutes, then beckoned him back.

"Going well," he said.

"Thanks," said Sid.

Mr Thorndon stroked Silver's neck. "Good on you, Silver. You make a champion of him, eh?" He squinted up at Sid. "I admire your determination, Sidney. But just remember, Rome wasn't built in a day. Hold your horses. You can't rush it."

Sid nodded. He wanted to say that actually, there was no time to spare, but he swallowed his words. "Yes, sir," he said.

"Good lad. I'll leave you to it. Are you going up the hill?"

"Yup."

"All right. Have fun," said Mr Thorndon.

Sid took the track to the hill. As he closed the last gate behind him, he breathed deep, and gazed around. Below him, the Thorndon's farm was like a picture from a children's book, with post and rail fences and neat paddocks, and big shade trees here and there. Next to the Thorndon's property, his parents' ten acres was a rough patch of grass surrounded by tōtara trees, with a muddle of old buildings in the middle of it. There was the woodpile, and Jess, lying in the sun. He grinned.

So funny, seeing it all from up here. You can tell rich from poor at a glance.

"Come on, Silver. Higher up!"

Silver trotted along the curve of the hill, then Sid urged him into a canter. He laughed out loud as the hillside became a blur of grass and earth, and the air rushed into his face, warm from the warm earth and full of the tang of the ocean. "Higher up, Silver, higher up!"

As if he also wanted a view from the highest point, Silver began heading for the top of the hill. He broke into a gallop, and Sid got himself whooping and hollering, shouting his head off. "What an idiot," he thought, then "nobody can hear me," and he went on yelling, alone on the hill, filled with the exhilaration of riding a horse that was as keen as he was, racing for the top.

At the top of the hill there was a small plateau, where the wind flattened the grass. Sid dismounted and walked Silver around, talking to him, before turning him loose to graze. He stood staring down at the view. The whole valley stretched below, the houses tiny, like painted wooden toys, their iron roofs a jumbled patchwork of red, green or rusty grey. Beyond the valley lay the sea, deep blue with crinkling waves and a brilliant white line of surf where the water met the land. The roar of the ocean carried faintly to his ears, and the shriek of seagulls pierced the distant dull crash and boom of waves on the sand.

A brilliant plan blossomed in his mind. Sid breathed deep, certainty sinking into his bones like an eel into a deep pool. Down there on the sand, he could go like the wind. Get up some real speed, thundering along beside the waves. No hills, no tussock grass, no ruts or sheep tracks. A clear run. His heart thudding, he turned and whistled for Silver.

"See the beach? Down there? Want to race with me along the sand?"

Silver dipped his head and whinnied. Sid laughed. "You're a funny one. I'll take that as a 'yes'. You'll love the beach. You're another Beach Dancer. Come on, back we go."

Remounting, he guided Silver back across the hillside and down the slope, walking now, listening to voices of the wind in the trees, and watching green and brown grasshoppers spring away from Silver's hooves into the rough, sun-browned grass.

They lost the sea breeze as they neared the farm, and hot, grass-scented air billowed up from the earth.

"Hello, Sid. Good ride?" said Mr Thorndon. He was standing at the bottom of the front steps to his house, looking like he was about to go inside.

"Yes, great!" said Sid.

"Go right up the hill?"

"Yes," said Sid. "You can see a long way up there."

"You certainly can," said Mr Thorndon. "Silver all right for you, do you think?"

"He's terrific." Sid hesitated. "Mr Thorndon?"

"Yes, Sidney?"

"What do you think about me riding him on the beach?"

"Well..." Mr Thorndon removed his hat and pushed his sandy hair back from his forehead. "I'm not saying that's not a good idea. The beach is a possibility. Can be dangerous, though."

"Yes," said Sid.

"Unpredictable, with storms and so forth. Driftwood washes up. Sometimes masses of it."

"Yes," said Sid again.

"But, you know... it's been settled weather for a while." Mr Thorndon lifted his gaze to the hills, turning his hat in his hands. Then he plonked it back onto his head, and gave Sid a bright, shrewd glance. "Give him a rub down, then. And turn him out into the paddock."

***

Sid rode home on Hugh, thinking hard.

It wasn't a 'no' about the beach. Not a 'yes' either. But near enough. Or is it? Riding on the beach without permission...

Guilt twisted in his gut, just thinking about it. He could never fool his ever-active conscience. But terrifying as it was to contemplate, it glowed in his mind like a bonfire at night. He'd be tempting fate, but that urgency was lodged in his bones, and he knew he must at least give it a go. How could he not? His blood was already racing with anticipation, and his tumbling thoughts turned into a plan.

The opportunity is right there on the doorstep, for goodness' sake. It's laid out for me. And what other options do I have? Just wait and see? No, I'd be mad not to try. And soon. I'll go tonight. It'll be a full moon. Nothing bad will happen. I wouldn't be doing anything really wrong. Not really wrong.

He lifted his chin, brushing away his worries, and nudged Hugh into a faster walk.

Chapter Ten

Night Riding

Awake in the dark, Sid listened to his brothers' breathing. Finally, they were asleep. He slipped out of bed, already dressed, and pulled on a jumper for warmth. Under the bed he had stowed his boots, wrapped in an old towel. He dragged them out. The bundle made a small, scuffing noise as it slid across the wooden floor. He tucked it under his arm and crept across to the door. The door handle squeaked. He held his breath, listening. Not a sound in the house. He closed the door and tiptoed towards the kitchen.

The back door was bolted. Was that usual? Sid eased out the bolt, willing it not to make a noise. Outside, he stood for a moment, breathing in the spicy night air, his face turned to the star-filled sky and the bright, full moon. Then he headed away from the house towards the cover of the tall pine trees.

His bare feet slipped on the thick layer of pine needles on the ground, still warm and fragrant from the long hot day. Jess brushed against his leg, wagging her tail.

"No, Jess. Go back," Sid whispered, finding it hard to have much authority in a whispered voice. "You can't come with me. Go back!"

Jess turned back and Sid pressed forward. The moonlight was so bright, everything appeared sharp and clear. The shadows were very black. Sid hurried past the barn and into the stand of prickly tōtara trees. He found Hugh's saddle and gear where he'd hidden them, and slung them over the rail fence into next door's paddock. Then he put on his boots and climbed over.

The Thorndon's horses were bunched in a group, disturbed by his sudden appearance. He would be taking Silver away from the safety of the herd. He might not like that.

"C'mon, Silver. It's me. You know me. We'll go for a bit of a ride, all right? A walk down the road."

Sid coaxed the horse into letting him put the halter on. "Good boy!" He laid the blanket on the horse's back and then the saddle. He tightened the girth. Then he led Silver to the gate and opened it. Together, they slipped out into the lane.

As they rounded the first bend, Sid glanced back. The other horses were watching them go, standing together in the moonlight. Silver whinnied.

"Come on Silver. You'll be all right. We'll be back soon."

The road to the beach seemed much longer than Sid had remembered. Silver's hooves beat out a steady rhythm on the dusty gravel road. Under the bright moon, it was almost like daylight. But there were dips and bends where overhanging trees blocked the moonlight, and the road disappeared into darkness. Sid found that if he didn't look directly ahead, he could just make out the glimmer of the gravel road, even in the darkest hollows. It was the peripheral vision trick that his dad had taught him years ago.

Sid knew they were getting closer. The muffled thunder of the surf grew louder with every turn, and the smell of salt was in the air. The road ended abruptly in rough grass. Sand dunes rose like a lumpy wall between the grass and the sea.

He rode up a small rise onto the hard-packed dunes, and the wind hit him full in the face. The waves roared, and there was the beach, spread out below.

Sid reined the horse in, gazing for a moment at the wild ocean. Then he nudged Silver with his heels, and they plunged down the glittering slope, through the dune grasses hissing and whispering in the wind, across deep, soft sand and onto the wide stretch of hard sand next to the sea, where a horse could run.

The tide was out. That was good. He hadn't thought about the tide. The roar of waves filled the air, and the foam churned and hissed at a distance. Sid gazed around. The sand sparkled in the moonlight. A small stream flowed away from the land, fanning out in rivulets towards the sea. A large log lay half buried, stranded there by a long-ago storm, its bleached limbs stretched high, gleaming white in the moonlight.

"Come on, boy." Sid leaned down and stroked Silver's neck. "Are you ready?"

He tapped his heels, and they splashed through the shallow stream. The horse seemed as eager as Sid to try the wide stretch of the shore. Trotting at first, then cantering, they moved faster and faster until they were galloping headlong. Sid laughed out loud as he sensed the power of the horse beneath him and felt the intoxication of speed. The roar of surf thundered in his ears and the drumming of hooves on the sand pounded through his body, making the blood race in his veins.

I reckon this is how flying feels!

It felt dangerous, almost frightening. But he felt protected, like nothing could hurt him. It was like a dream. Like flying through moonlight. He felt the horse's excitement, the way he strained forward, the effortless movement of his muscles.

"You love this, don't you, Silver?" he shouted.

He slowed the horse and turned him. "Silver! It's great, isn't it? It'll build up your stamina. Mine too. It's what we need. It's what we were born for."

He leaned forward, stroking the horse's neck, and spoke in a low voice. "Silver? This is our secret. We're in training. Or I am. And you're helping me. But my dad wouldn't like it, so he can't know. I want to be a famous jockey, but he doesn't want me to. And I don't really know why." He paused. "And I have to help my sister. She needs to finish school and be a teacher. So, if I could earn some money..." He sighed. "Anyway, that's why it's really important." He glanced around and shivered. "Just so you know. Alright? Time to go back now."

They had come a long way. So far, he couldn't see where they'd started from. All the shoreline looked the same. "I suppose we'll know it when we see it. The way home, I mean. And we can follow our tracks." As he began trotting back along the beach, a few wisps of cloud drifted across the moon. He slowed the horse to a walk. "Beautiful, eh Silver? Funny to think that everybody's asleep. Nobody sees this. We're the only ones awake." Silver snorted and shook his head, and Sid stroked his neck. "Come on, then."

They cantered back. The dead tree loomed ahead, gleaming white in the darkness.

That's the tree.

He slowed Silver to a walk again. They crossed the small stream, passed the tree, and headed for the dunes.

Powdery sand flew up in little puffs as they reached the top. Sid stopped the horse and looked back. The waves thundered and roared below. The sand shone silver in the moonlight, and the small stream carved a black pattern on its way to the sea. He could see their tracks clearly in the sand. The dead tree reared up stiff and stark, a reminder of what the wild storms on the coast could do.

That's where we started from. Should be easy to remember.

***

The ride back seemed much quicker, and the dark corners were less scary. Sid was elated. "We did it, Silver!" At the gate, he dismounted and led Silver back into the paddock. He removed the bridle and saddle and hunted under the hedge for the old towel. "Sorry I can't brush you down, boy. But I'll give you a good rub."

He towelled the horse all over, making sure he was dry. Then he hid the horse gear under the hedge and slipped back through the trees. The barn and the house were dark and silent. Jess met him, wagging her tail. He opened the back door, stepped inside and quietly re-bolted it. He felt suddenly dead-tired.

As he opened his bedroom door, one of the twins stirred. "Sid? You back?"

"Yeah, I'm back. Did I wake you up?"

"Nah. I woke up before, and you were gone." Bill's voice was sleepy. "I was worried, Sid."

"Nothing to worry about," said Sid. "It was great. I'm real tired now, though."

"Is the horse back in the paddock?"

"Yes, he's back." Sid climbed into bed. "He's fine, Bill. He loved it."

"That's good. Good night, Sid."

"Good night, Bill." Sid listened to his brother turn over, and heard his breathing settle to a steady rhythm. He yawned.

That was amazing. But it seems unreal now. And I'm exhausted. How long can I keep doing this?

A nagging guilt made his stomach clench, but he pushed it aside.

I'm not doing anything wrong. Mr Thorndon didn't actually say I mustn't ride on the beach.

He thought of something else.

And how long can I keep it secret? How long before some-body finds out what I'm doing? Dad always seems to discover everything.

Chapter Eleven

Fight at School

Sid glanced around the classroom. No Beryl. His heart sank every time he saw her empty seat. She'd be in Miller's, selling buttons and lace and elastic. He seldom had a chance to speak to her these days. He avoided looking at Sarah. One glimpse of Sarah and guilt gnawed and squirmed inside him like a rat in a barrel of apples. In broad daylight, the night riding seemed insane.

What if she ever found out? What if her father found out?

His head hurt. Mr Cowley kept them working hard all morning, and as a reward, he was going to read to the class before lunch. Great Expectations. Very apt. Or ironic. Desk lids banged as everyone put their work away.

Mr Cowley opened the book. "Everyone sitting comfortably? Now, where were we last time?"

Usually, Sid loved listening, but today he just wanted to put his head down on the desk and fall asleep. Sid tried to stay awake, but his eyelids kept closing. He felt Rick's elbow in his side.

"Don't fall asleep."

"Shut up, Rick, I'm all right."

***

The scraping of chairs on the wooden floor jerked Sid awake. He scrambled to join the class as they shuffled and pushed their way to the cloakroom to get their lunches.

"Nice sleep?" Rick was right behind him, breathing in his ear. "Couldn't help noticing, mate. Your snoring gave you away."

"I don't snore," said Sid.

"No?"

"Just shut up, Rick."

"Alright, you didn't snore," said Rick. "But your head kept clunking down like it was going to fall off your neck. It was painful to watch."

The boys grabbed their lunches and hurried outside. Sid unwrapped his sandwiches. They were the usual—limp lettuce and marmite. He normally wolfed them down, but today he was so tired he could hardly even look at them.

Rick eyed him anxiously. "What's the matter? Are you tired from working after school?"

"No," said Sid. "Well, yes. But it's not that."

"What then?" said Rick.

"What do you mean?" asked Sid.

"You can hardly keep your eyes open," said Rick. "What are you up to?"

Sid had been expecting it. Rick knew him too well. "You have to keep quiet about it," he said.

"If you say so."

Sid took a deep breath and straightened his shoulders. "You mustn't tell *anyone*."

***

"Shhh, Rick, do you want everybody to hear?"

"Nobody's listening." Rick crumpled his sandwich paper. "Sid, you must be mad. You'll be in so much trouble if anything goes wrong."

"Nothing's going to go wrong," said Sid.

"What if the horse has an accident? Remember Glenys?"

"I'm not Glenys," said Sid. "I used to ride Hugh on the beach all the time."

"You're going to fall asleep in a lesson, and old Cowley's gonna roar. He's not stupid - he can see who's listening and who isn't."

"I can handle it," said Sid.

"You'll get sick."

"You're an old granny," said Sid.

"I just don't want to see you get into trouble," said Rick.

"Speaking of trouble," said Sid, "here it comes now."

Roger Dyson swaggered up, his mates trailing after him. "Morning, Everett. Sleep well? In class, I mean?"

Sid bristled. The memory of Roger spooking the Captain's horse was still fresh in his mind. "Shut up, Dyson."

"Oh, grumpy, are we?" Roger smirked. "Sorry, didn't mean to provoke. Just concerned. Thought you must be working too hard. Hoeing turnips."

Sid leaped to his feet. "What did you say?" His fists were up before he knew it. "Just say that again, Dyson."

"You heard me. Hoeing turnips. Rather tiring, I imagine." Roger grinned around at his followers. "Enough to make you fall asleep in class, anyway. Thought you loved Great Expectations. You missed a good chapter."

"I heard it."

"You heard yourself snoring."

"That's it, Dyson," Sid shouted. "You want a go? Well, you've got one."

Roger backed off and put his fists up. A circle of boys instantly formed around them, their eager voices shouting encouragement. Sid narrowed his eyes and jabbed out, landing a hard punch in Roger's chest. Roger stumbled back, then lurched forward and swung. Sid thought he heard his ribs crack before they crashed to the ground together, rolling and punching.

Rage exploded in Sid's head as months of frustration boiled up inside him. He could hear the crowd of boys around them yelling. Dirt and stones pressed into his knees and scraped his shins, and he tasted blood in his mouth. A close view of Roger's face made him almost laugh, the situation seemed so ridiculous, but he was bursting with anger and his arms were fired with strength he didn't know he had.

Someone shouted, "Teacher's coming! Watch out!"

Sid sensed, rather than saw, the crowd scatter. Too furious to stop, and knowing that Roger was weakening, he kept on punching.

"Boys! Boys, stop that at once!" Mr Cowley was standing over them. "At once! Stand up, both of you."

Sid and Roger, dishevelled and bleeding, scrambled to their feet and stood glaring at each other.

"That'll do," said Mr Cowley. "To the office. Now."

The tiny school didn't have a headmaster. Mr Cowley did the honours. He closed the door with a click. There had been no time for Sid to pad his shorts with newspaper.

Mr Cowley took out the cane. "You first, Sidney. Bend over."

Sid bent over, hands on his knees, arms braced and teeth clenched, waiting for the thwack of the cane, and the pain. The air seemed to vibrate as the cane swished down, once, twice, three times. Sid kept his mouth shut, gritting his teeth, determined not to make a sound. Then he stood stiffly and stumbled across the room to stand against the wall and watch as Roger Dyson bent over for his turn.

Sid's heart pounded. He felt ill as he listened to the swish of the cane and the sharp smack as it landed. Once, twice, three times. He watched in a daze as Roger stood, his face tear-streaked, and realised that tears were running down his own cheeks.

Mr Cowley surveyed the pair of them, grim-faced. "All right, boys?"

"Yes, sir."

"Yes, Mr Cowley."

"Good. Then you can go, and not waste any more of my time than you already have." He frowned. "And let's have no more of this nonsense. I expect much better from you boys. You'll be seniors next year. You can start acting like it now."

Outside, Roger hurried off without a word. Sid spotted Rick waiting for him under an oak tree on the side of the field. Tiredly, he wandered over. "Thanks for waiting."

"That's all right," said Rick.

Sid leaned his back against the tree. "I suppose the bell's going to ring any minute."

"Yes." Rick paused. "Does he know what it was about?"

"Rick, I don't even know what it was about." Sid scuffed his foot on the dusty ground below the oak tree. "That Roger just annoys me so much. How did he find out about hoeing turnips?"

"At least he doesn't suspect the real reason you're tired," said Rick.

"Yeah. I suppose turnip hoeing is the perfect cover." Sid gave a crooked smile. "The only good thing in my life at the moment is riding Silver."

"If it really is a good thing," said Rick.

"It has to be," said Sid.

"And a certain girl?" Rick asked.

Sid felt his face flush, and again the rat writhed in his stomach. "Rick, what if she finds out I'm riding one of their horses on the beach? I've got permission to ride in the paddock, and up on the hills, but they have no idea I'm going all the way to the beach and riding him on the sand. If they ever find out..."

"I think it's time to stop," said Rick. "Pack it in." He narrowed his eyes, assessing his friend's face. "And you'd better clean yourself up before class."

Sid looked down at himself. His shirt was torn, his knees were grazed and muddy. "Not much I can do about the shirt," he said. "I'll be in trouble about that."

Together they walked to the boys' toilets, and Sid splashed cold water onto his face. He wet his handkerchief and carefully began to wipe away the blood and mud from his knees.

"I can't stop now," he said.

"Why not?" said Rick. "You're not doing yourself any favours."

"No," said Sid. "I've got to keep going."

"Why?" asked Rick.

"I need to train."

Rick sighed. "You need to train."

"Yes." Sid rinsed his handkerchief under the tap. "And Silver loves it. It's building his muscles up. He's getting more confident, too. Really fired up and keen. Mr Thorndon said he'd lost his drive. Well, I think he's got it back."

"Okay, so quit now."

"No," said Sid.

"Why not? It's stupid. You're exhausted."

"It's the only way." Sid examined his knees, stinging from the cold water. Then he walked stiffly out of the toilet block and into the sunshine.

Rick followed him. "There's always another way."

"Well, I can't think of one." Sid glared at his friend. "I'm not going to give up. I'm going to be a top jockey, Rick. I'll make lots of money. You'll see. I'm going to be famous."

"Yeah. I guess I'll see," said Rick. "If you live long enough. I don't expect you'll be doing any riding tonight, though."

"No." Sid was only too aware of the pain that would make even riding home pretty uncomfortable.

The bell rang, and they turned and walked back towards the classroom.

Sid sighed. "Maybe you're right, Rick. I don't know how long I can keep this up. I'm not hoeing turnips today, anyway. That's for sure." He avoided looking at anyone as they approached the classroom. "Dad will ask why when he gets home."

"Don't let your dad give you a hard time," said Rick.

"Not much I can do about that," said Sid.

Chapter Twelve

Ruby

"Mum, I'm home!" Sid pushed the kitchen door open. "I didn't go to work with Dad. I..." Sid broke off. "Mum, what's wrong?"

"Oh Sid, sit down a minute, and hold Ruby," said Mum. "I just got home and I'm so upset." Mum's face was pale. Her hair was floating out from under her hat. She paused and stared at Sid's battered appearance and grazed knees. "What on earth has happened to you? You haven't been fighting?"

"Never mind that," said Sid. "Mum, you sit down, and you hold Ruby. I'll make a cup of tea."

Sid hunted around. He found a box of matches, glancing over his shoulder all the time at his mother's white face. His stomach clenched. "Mum, what happened? Was there an accident?"

"There almost was. Oh, I can't believe it happened. Or didn't happen. It almost did. Oh Sid, Ruby!" She clutched Ruby, who appeared unconcerned. She was sucking her thumb though—a sure sign of tiredness or worry.

Sid lit the small kerosene stove and made the tea, peering over at his mother now and again. The cup rattled in the saucer as he carried it across the room. "Here, Mum. I put some sugar in it."

"Thanks Sid, I don't mind if I do, for once."

"So, tell me." Sid sat opposite his mother, gazing into her face. "Mum, let me take your hat." He pulled out the hatpin and handed it to Ruby. "Here you go, Ruby." He smiled into her serious eyes. "The giant pearl. You like this one, Rubes."

She took it and twirled it in her fingers, a smile touching the corners of her mouth. She rubbed the smooth surface of the pearl against her cheek. "Moo."

"Yeah, smooth. Very good, Rubes." Sid took it from her, and lifted his mother's hat from her head. He placed the hat on the sideboard and stuck the pin into a pincushion.

"It doesn't go there, Sid," said Mum.

"I know. It doesn't matter." He handed her the cup and saucer. "Here, Mum. Now tell me."

"Well." She blinked several times. "I was in town, with Ruby. And I was talking to Mrs Bridges about, I don't know, nothing important. You know how she goes on. And Ruby wandered off. She knows, she absolutely knows not to go on the road, but she must have, because suddenly there was this screeching of brakes and a huge honking of a horn and this enormous car almost ran her over. Right before my eyes. I had a feeling something was wrong, and I turned around and there she was, in the road. And there was this enormous car."

She stopped. Sid touched her arm. "Go on. What happened next? Ruby's all right."

"Yes, the car didn't hit her. But it could have. Oh Sid, I would never have forgiven myself if Ruby had got hurt." She took a gulping breath. "And then the driver got out and started yelling at me. Told me I needed to control my daughter, and I don't remember what else he said, he just yelled. I didn't say anything, I was so shocked. Then his wife got out of the car, and she was lovely. She took Ruby by the hand and led her back to me, and she put her arm around me and said it could happen to anyone."

"Sounds like a nice lady," said Sid.

"She was very nice. She asked me how old Ruby was and what her name was. But her husband! I supposed he was in shock, I don't know." She paused. "But you know what, Sid? It wouldn't have happened to anyone. Not to most people. Unless they had a tiny child, and then they'd be watching. It happened to us because Ruby is deaf. She didn't hear the car. And I'm so used to her being quite grown up now, even though she's only little. I mean, she manages so well, I never thought she'd do that. I didn't think it for a moment. She could have died, Sid."

Mum took a sip of her tea. "Anyway, I told them that Ruby was deaf, and they went all quiet and looked at me. And then they looked at each other. And then they got into their car and drove away."

Mum put down her cup and saucer and picked up her handbag. "And Sid, I've been hiding this letter." She took it out of her handbag. "It's that one from the Ministry of Education. About Ruby. I can't leave it anywhere in the house; Dad might find it. He's forgotten about it, and I don't want to remind him. I still haven't answered it. I've been carrying it around in my bag."

Sid took the letter. "You didn't answer it?"

"No. And procrastination won't solve anything. But the local school won't work for Ruby. And Deaf School... it's just—the distance."

"Yeah, Beryl told me. Christchurch or Auckland. Opposite ends of the country. And we live right in the middle."

"The deaf children used to have to go to Australia, so at least it's not that far away. But still, she's so little. How do other parents cope with it?"

The back door banged, and the twins came in.

"Mum, what's up?" The twins crowded around her. "Are you crying?"

Sid answered for her. "Ruby almost got run over in town."

"Really? What happened?" Their faces were eager.

Mum gave a shaky laugh. "Not now, boys. I just told it all to Sid." She blinked the tears away. "Let's just say she's all right."

The twins looked disappointed.

Mum smiled at them. "I'll tell you what you can do to help, boys. Take Ruby outside and feed the chickens, and she can collect the eggs. The basket's on the dresser."

The boys dragged Ruby outside. Mum sighed with relief. "She loves finding the eggs. And it makes the day feel normal again."

Normal again? Dad's boots sounded on the front porch.

"Quick, give me the letter, Sid," said Mum. She slipped it back into her handbag. "I need more time to think."

"What does Beryl say about it?" asked Sid.

"She knows Ruby has to go. Very keen on education, our Beryl."

"Yeah, she was." Sid felt his anger rising again. "Now look at her."

"She's not stupid, Sid," said Mum. "Beryl knows what she's doing. She wants to help, and she's doing what she thinks is right. There's always more than one way to look at things."

Dad banged the door open. "Sidney? Why weren't you at the farm after school?"

"I had to stay late," said Sid.

"And why was that?" Dad asked.

Mum frowned, turning to Sid. "I didn't think about that, Sidney. You should have come home with your father." Her eyes went to Sid's knees and his torn shirt. "And look at the state of you!"

"It was nothing. Just school." Sid thought fast. "Dad, Mum has something to tell you."

Dad's eyes moved from Sid's face to his wife's. "What?" he asked.

Mum looked at Sid. "Any more tea in that pot?"

"Oh, yeah," said Sid. "I'll get you a cup of tea, Dad." He hurried to the bench and found another cup and saucer and then found the milk. He didn't want to turn around in case his dad was watching him.

Behind him, he heard Dad's voice, sounding surprisingly gentle. "So, Mary, what's happened?"

Sid glanced over his shoulder at his parents. Dad was actually holding Mum's hand. He quickly looked away and got busy with the teapot and strainer. They weren't talking at all. He glanced around again. Dad was still holding Mum's hand and looking into her eyes. As he watched, Mum's tears spilled out and ran down her cheeks.

"I'm all right, Arthur," said Mum. "I'll be fine. It was just an awful shock."

Sid poured out a cup of tea and carried it across to where his parents were sitting.

"Here you are, Dad. Cup of tea."

Dad didn't move, so Sid put the cup and saucer on the table and tiptoed to the back door.

Outside, he leaned against the wall and breathed in the soft, pine-scented air. He could hear the boys calling the chickens, banging the bucket with a spoon. The sky was pale gold between the tree trunks on the ridge, arching to soft grey-blue overhead, and the moon was already visible.

Sid sighed. The moon was waning. His mind wandered to the riding gear hidden under the tōtara trees. Not tonight, anyway. He was in too much pain to ride tonight. Maybe tomorrow night. He should be able to do one more night, at least. Perhaps two, if the weather stayed fine. There was a storm moving up from the South Island, apparently.

Gotta do as many nights as I can, while I've still got the moon. And before the storm hits.

Chapter Thirteen

Almost Caught

The sweat was cooling on Sid's back as he dismounted in the lane. He opened the gate to the Thorndon's paddock. His whole body was aching. He began to shiver and couldn't stop. "There you go, Silver. Back again." Wearily he led Silver through onto the wet grass and closed the gate, his hands fumbling with the latch. Tiredness made every task difficult. His hands shook as he groped under the hedge for the towel. He pulled it out. It was damp with dew.

"C'mon, Silver. Let's give you a rubdown."

For the last two nights of this week, he had willed himself to stay awake, fighting his tiredness, to creep next door and take Silver along the moonlit road to the beach. The last two nights were the hardest. He had forced himself to make the most of the moonlight while it lasted. Now exhaustion had caught up with him. Swaying on his feet, and still shivering uncontrollably, Sid longed to sink down into the grass, wet though it was, and sleep.

"Here you go, boy." Sid rubbed the horse all over. His arms ached, the muscles in his legs ached, his whole body longed for rest.

Hardly noticing the scratchy tōtara branches, Sid groped his way through the trees and climbed over the fence. A rooster crowed. Almost morning. Something snagged his clothes, and a sharp pain stabbed through his leg. Reaching down, his fingers touched barbed wire. He must have come the wrong way. He unhooked his torn trousers and went on.

Crossing the garden towards the house, he suddenly stopped. He could smell cigarette smoke. Unmistakably. That meant—he froze. Dad must be out here, smoking. But where?

Sid's heart was pounding. He listened. The wind was rising, stirring the branches of the trees, and rustling their leaves. A morepork called somewhere nearby. With careful steps, he crept forward, afraid that every move was taking him into danger. His tired muscles strained to move as silently as possible, but he knew that weariness was making him clumsy. He couldn't think clearly—fear and tiredness seemed to short-circuit his brain. All he wanted was to get inside and into bed.

As he reached the house, he froze again. Right in front of him, the orange glow of a cigarette flared and faded. Dad was standing by the back door.

"Out late, son."

"Dad," said Sid.

"Where have you been?" Dad asked.

"Um..." Sid's mouth was dry, and no words came.

The cigarette flared again. Dad's eyes gleamed in the orange glow, his eyebrows a bushy line above them.

"You going to tell me?"

Sid was silent. His heart pounded. He felt a trickle of blood run down his leg.

Dad dropped the cigarette stub on the ground, where it threw out a couple of sparks onto the dirt path. He ground it into the dust with his boot. "Doesn't matter, boy." Dad spoke slowly. "You don't have to tell me. I'll find out one day. It doesn't matter. Things are going to change now. Change for a bit, anyhow."

"Going to change, Dad?" Sid felt dizzy. His brain didn't seem to take things in like it should.

"I'm going to Auckland, Sidney. For a funeral."

"A funeral?" Sid asked.

"Nobody you know. Someone from the army. Another one of my mates, gone. I'll be away for a week, at least." Dad moved aside. "In you go, Sidney."

Sid stumbled to his room, feeling his shirt sticking to his back, his sweat now cold and clammy. Without getting changed, he crawled into bed and curled up, shivering. Every muscle ached. When he closed his eyes, he heard the hiss and roar of waves, and saw the moonlit beach. He was falling asleep almost immediately. If only he could stop shivering.

Maybe I'm getting sick. He leaned over the side of the bed and found his jacket on the floor. He spread it out on the top of the bed, over his quilt, trying to get a bit more warmth. Dad's words were spinning in his head—'away for a week, at least.'

That would be nice. A break from Dad. Sid hoped he wouldn't hurry back. He felt guilty even as he thought it.

True, though. He closed his eyes again.

"Sid?" Bruce's voice came from the other side of the room. "Sid, are you back?"

"Yeah, I'm here," said Sid.

"Are you all right?"

"I'm freezing!"

"It's not cold," said Bruce.

"It's cold outside. Anyway, I'm freezing. I think I might be getting sick."

"Were you talking to Dad outside?" asked Bruce.

"Yeah, I was."

"Did he catch you?" The fear in Bruce's voice wasn't hard to miss.

"He saw me coming back. He gave me a huge fright. Did you know he's going to Auckland?"

"What for?" asked Bruce.

"A funeral. Someone from the army," said Sid.

"Oh. No, I didn't know about that." Bruce rustled around, rearranging his pillow. "Well, I'm going back to sleep. Good night, Sid."

"Good night, Bruce." Sid turned over, his leg hurting. His trouser leg was sticking to the blood. He hoped it didn't leak through onto the sheets. Mum would be mad. She had a thing about blood—it was hard to wash out of things. His shivering began to ease off. He shook his pillow, then sank his head into it.

Get some sleep. That's all that mattered. Tomorrow, Dad was going away. How wonderful!

Outside, tree branches scraped and tapped against the window as the wind gathered strength.

Chapter Fourteen

Dad's Back

"Dad's back, Dad's back!"

The twins were dancing around, as though having Dad back again was the greatest thing ever. Jess was barking and jumping around as though Dad had been gone for ages, not just for a few days. He had returned earlier than he'd said. Sid wondered why.

Mum was smiling, Ruby was laughing her loud, funny laugh that made everyone else laugh too.

And Dad was beaming. Sid couldn't take his eyes off him, he seemed so different. He looked years younger. He'd never seen his dad so happy since the day he first came back from the war. Dad took off his hat, threw it across the room, and hoisted Ruby up into the air, whirling her around until she shrieked. He laughed and sat down, with Ruby, grinning, on his knee.

"Gather 'round, everyone." Sid realised Dad was bursting with news. "I've got something to tell you all. It'll change our lives. It'll change everything."

"What, my dear?" Mum's eyes were bright. Sid thought he could read apprehension, as well as hope, shining there.

"I've got a job. In Auckland," said Dad.

"A job? What?" Mum sat down all of a sudden.

"At a mill, in Henderson. That's west of Auckland."

"At a mill?" said Mum. "A proper job?"

"A proper job. Full time. Good pay." Dad took a deep breath and exhaled in a long sigh. "I can't believe it."

"That's wonderful," said Mum. Her voice sounded sort of shaky, like she might cry. "Truly? Tell us all about it." She caught Sid's eye. "Sidney? Put the kettle on."

"Well," said Dad. "I stayed with my friend Ernie. He was in my regiment. And he works at this mill. Big mill. With a water wheel and everything. Lots of men working there. So, he says to me, have you got any work down there? And I said no, not much. Told him about the turnips. So he says, there's lots of work here, and I'm going to ask for you. And he did. And I'm hired."

Mum gasped. "Just like that?"

"Just like that." Dad rubbed his chin. "I met the manager. Nice bloke. And it's all settled."

"So..." he gazed around at their expectant faces. "We're moving."

"Moving?" The word burst out; Sid couldn't help himself.

"Yup.," said Dad. "The whole family. Sell the cows. Get rid of the chooks. Shifting the whole family up to the big smoke."

"Oh Arthur. That'll mean... Oh, Arthur! It's the end of all our worries!" Mum's smile was the biggest Sid had ever seen on her face.

"Yes. School for Ruby. Beryl, you can quit your old drapery shop. Come up to Auckland and get a better job. Or go to school there. Finish your schooling, and you can be a teacher, after all."

"Oh, Dad!" Beryl's eyes were bright.

Sid surveyed his family. Bill's hair was sticking up. Bruce's shirt was inside out. He tried to imagine them in Auckland.

But never mind the twins. What about his own dreams?

"Dad?" he asked. His father peered over at him, and he felt his heart begin to thump. "Um, are there horses up there?"

"Horses?" said Dad.

Sid looked at him. He must know something.

"Yes, of course there are," said Dad. "Henderson's full of horses. There'll be something in the horse line, I suppose. But school, that's what you need. Or if they want to take on a boy, you can work at the mill. My mate'll put a word in for you."

Mum picked Ruby up and began dancing around the room with her. Ruby giggled and shrieked as Mum whirled her around. She would have no idea why everyone was so happy. She just lit up when everyone else did.

Sid warmed the pot, put the tea leaves in and added the boiling water. Then he stood in a daze. Beryl handed him the knitted tea cosy. He took it from her, unseeing. Put it on the teapot the wrong way round. Stood thinking.

I'll have to say something.

Beryl pushed him away and turned the cosy the right way around. She set out the best cups and saucers, glanced at Mum, then took down the cake tin with the last of the Christmas cake in it.

Sid stepped forward. "Dad?"

"Yes, Sidney?" Dad's voice was wary.

Sid felt sweat starting on his forehead. "Dad, I'm going to leave school as soon as I can." He spoke carefully. "And Dad?"

"Go on, son."

"I was planning to ask Mr Thorndon for work. If I got it, I wouldn't have to go with you. To Auckland."

"You mean an apprenticeship?" asked Dad.

"Yes," said Sid.

"You know what I think about that."

"Not really." Sid felt his face getting hotter. What exactly did his father have against him becoming a jockey?

"You need a real job for the real world, son," said Dad. HIs face had hardened. "Dreams are free when you're a boy, Sidney. But when you're a man..." He straightened his shoulders. "You have to take what you can get."

"But Dad," Sid burst out, "what if I can get the apprenticeship?"

"Has he offered you one?"

"No," said Sid.

"Has he led you to believe that he will offer you one? In the near future?"

"Sort of," said Sid.

"Sort of." Dad shook his head. "Then it's dreaming, Sidney. It's pie in the sky. It's not real. Nothing's real if it isn't actually happening."

"But—when you have a plan—when you know it's possible..."

"You don't know that, Sid." Dad's voice got a hard edge to it. "You don't know it's possible. I know what's possible. Work at the mill, or finish your schooling. Either way, you're coming with us."

Sid turned away. Beryl was watching him with a pitying sort of look. He couldn't stand that. Desperate to get outside, he left them to their tea and cake and rushed to the back door.

As he opened it, a tremendous gust of wind caught the door and swung it so that it banged. He grabbed a jacket, pulled the hood over his head, and slipped outside. The wind roared in his ears, and the tops of the trees whipped around. He staggered across the yard. The scratch on his leg hadn't healed, and it throbbed with every step. He climbed through the fence into Hugh's paddock, and buried his face in Hugh's mane, breathing in the comforting smell of horse.

"Hugh, my boy." A surge of affection choked him up. "Hugh! I can't leave you behind."

And what about Silver, and the night riding?

Even as he thought it, he realised he'd had enough of night riding. It had done him well. He was confident, and fast. Silver was brilliant, and they were a great team. But what next? Maybe in Henderson, there would be an opportunity to get closer to his goal. They must have horse racing in Auckland.

But then, what about Sarah?

His stomach lurched, and something like real, actual pain shot through him. He knew for certain he didn't want to leave Sarah. Leave her to Roger? He didn't think so. Not that she cared anything about Roger anyway, he was pretty sure about that. "Smarmy," he muttered. He stepped back from Hugh. "Yeah, smarmy. I'm not leaving. I'm not leaving you, Hugh. And I'm not leaving Sarah. And that's that."

A voice called from the house. "Sidney!"

It was Beryl.

"Yes?" he answered.

"Do you want a cup of tea?"

"No, thank you."

"Are you sure?" she asked.

"Yes, I'm sure." He shouted louder than he needed to.

Beryl came across the yard, head bent against the wind, and stood at the fence. "Sid, you don't want to go, do you?"

"No, I don't."

"It's an amazing opportunity," she said. "For all of us."

"Yeah," said Sid. "And I'm really happy for you. I just... can't they leave me behind?"

"I'm pretty sure they can't, Sid," said Beryl, "and they won't. Perhaps if you'd started a job. But you haven't. You're still at school."

"Well, I'm not going. I'll find a way to stay here," said Sid.

"Don't get your hopes up." She eyed him sternly. "And Sid, Mum's thrilled about it. She's really excited, for the first time in ages. So don't spoil it for her."

"I won't," he said.

Beryl glanced up at the sky. Black clouds had covered the sun. "Better get the cows milked before it pours."

"Yeah. I'll get the bucket." He grimaced. "Milking the cows is one thing I wouldn't mind saying goodbye to."

Sid collected the milk bucket and billy and put on an old raincoat. He searched for a hat, then gave up. As he headed up the track to the hill where the cows were grazing, the rain began. Stinging, cold drops drove into his face as he climbed the slope, his feet slipping on the stones, the clay turning to mud almost instantly.

He reached the top paddock and stared around. Where were they? The wind buffeted him, and raindrops drummed on his raincoat. Water dripped into his eyes, from his wet hair. He peered through the sheets of rain driving across the hilltop and spotted the cows standing under a couple of trees. Their heads were bent low, their tails turned to the wind. They wouldn't take kindly to being moved in this weather. He hobbled across the rough grass towards them.

"Come on. Milking time."

They huddled together, shifting further in under the trees.

Sid swore under his breath. "Come on, you stupid cows. I'm getting wet. It'll be dry in the shed." He got around behind them, waving his arms. "Shoo! Move it!"

They kicked up their heels, suddenly, and ran out into the rain, udders bouncing and tails swishing around. Sid ran after them. He chased them down the hill, his feet slipping and sliding. He penned them in, then hurried to get Hugh to bring him in out of the rain. Hugh followed him gladly into the barn.

Sid gave him some hay. "There you go, Hugh. Nice and dry in here." He stroked Hugh's neck. "Suppose I'd better get those cows milked."

As he stepped outside, the wind caught the barn door. He felt it smack hard onto the side of his head. He saw stars, and then everything went black.

Chapter Fifteen

Holding Sarah's Horse

"Sit by the fire, Sid." Mum shifted a pile of clean washing. "It's good to see you looking better. The doctor said you might be a week, and it's been almost three."

"The doctor. Yeah. He bandaged my head." And he had shone a light into his eyes, Sid remembered, and asked a lot of questions. He'd been quite cross about the scratch on his leg. "He was really grumpy with me."

"I don't blame him," said Mum. "He was worried about concussion. And it horrified him that you'd said nothing about your leg. So then I felt terrible I hadn't known how bad it was. You told me it was just a scratch."

"It was." Sid sank into an armchair. He sensed her eyes on him, studying his face.

"It could have been tetanus, Sid," said Mum. "You could have died. Lucky for you, it was just infected, but the doctor said it was pretty serious."

Sid stretched his legs, resting his feet on the warm bricks next to the coal range, soaking up the heat through his woollen socks. His leg was still stiff, but the pain had gone. "Sorry, Mum. Anyway, it's fine now." He grinned at her. "Actually, it's quite nice, being an invalid. Think I'll keep it up as long as I can!"

"If you say things like that, it won't be for long." She rumpled his hair. "Shows you're feeling better, anyway." She sat down on a kitchen chair next to him. "You gave us a huge fright. Your father had to carry you back across from the barn. Lucky he's a strong man."

Sid had a hazy memory of being picked up and carried. And he remembered Dad saying something like he was a good boy for looking after his horse. A wave of emotion flooded through him. He was grateful to Dad for finding him and carrying him back, but he was also angry that he'd made him go up the hill to fetch the cows in the first place.

"Nobody knew it was a storm coming, Sid." Mum sometimes seemed to know what he was thinking.

"I knew." Sid gazed into the firebox, watching the flames flicker and dance around the lumps of wood. Was it really three weeks ago? It seemed much longer since that last ride before the weather broke.

"Sidney," said Mum, "would you like to go into town for me? It's a lovely day, and it'd do you good to get out. You could have a nice ride on Hugh. I'm sure he's missed you." Mum narrowed her eyes, assessing him. "I think you're well enough. You could visit Beryl. She'd like that. She's been worried about you."

"How's she finding it at Mrs Archibald's?" Sid asked.

"All right, I think," said Mum.

"It must be funny, boarding with someone else," said Sid.

"She needed to do it," said Mum. "It's quite a walk into Foxton." Mum sighed. "Mrs Archibald is a nice lady. I miss Beryl, though. It's been awfully quiet, with her gone, and you in bed."

"Quiet? With the twins and Ruby?" Sid smiled. "Yup, I'll go in. I'll ride Hugh. I couldn't walk in, that's for sure."

***

At the picnic grounds, Sid dismounted and tied Hugh to the railing. "I won't be long, Hugh." He walked to the main street. His leg was stiff, and he had to try hard to move normally. He felt sort of dazed. People's voices and the roar of motor car engines seemed extra loud. The aroma of fresh bread wafted in the air, and he stopped in front of the bakery window. Puffy loaves stood in a row, each with a strip of tissue paper around the middle. The smell made him hungry, even though he'd eaten breakfast not long ago. Currant buns with shiny glazed tops caught his eye. He searched in his pocket for some money.

One for me, one for Beryl.

At the drapery shop, Sid hesitated. The shop bell jangled as someone came out. He peered through the doorway. Beryl stood behind the counter, her hair up, wearing her long-sleeved black shop dress. It surprised him to see how different she looked. She appeared... grown up. He pushed the door wide open and went in.

"Sid!" Beryl rushed out from behind the counter and crushed him in a hug. "Sid! You're all right!" She held him at arm's length and examined his face. "Yeah," she grinned and gave him a punch. "You look fine. C'mon, I'll ask if we can go outside." She turned and called out, "Mrs Archibald?"

The shop owner poked her head out of the office.

"Mrs Archibald, is it alright if I go out for a few minutes with my brother?"

"Of course, dear." Mrs Archibald studied Sid. "Been in the wars, then? How's the head?"

"It's better now, thanks, Mrs Archibald."

"That's good to hear," she said.

In the street, Sid handed Beryl her currant bun. "Special delivery."

"Yum! Thanks, Sid!" She held up the bun, turning it so that the sugar glaze shone in the sun. Then she looked over her shoulder. "Hey, horses coming. And look who it is! Mr Thorndon. And guess who else?" She elbowed her brother.

Sid glanced up quickly and felt his face flush. Sarah was riding next to her father. She was on Talley, her new pony. He didn't have time to think of a clever greeting, or to hide his bun.

"Good morning, Sid. How are you?" Sarah pulled her horse up and sat smiling down at him.

"Good morning, Sarah," said Sid.

"Hello, young man." Mr Thorndon stopped beside his daughter. "Late breakfast?" Sid didn't know what to say. He held the sticky bun awkwardly. Mr Thorndon smiled. "Glad to see you're up and about. Heard about your accident."

"Thank you, sir," said Sid.

"We're just out for a ride. Lovely morning," Mr Thorndon said.

"Yes," said Sid.

"Sid!" Sarah's forehead crinkled up with concern. "I heard your accident was really bad."

"I'm fine," said Sid. "It was just the storm. The barn door hit me."

"Come on, Sarah," said Mr Thorndon. "Let's keep moving."

"All right, Dad." She smiled at Sid. "Good to see you, Sid."

"Yeah, you too."

As they rode off, Beryl started to giggle.

"Shhh, you idiot!" Sid turned on her. "They'll hear you!"

"No, they won't," said Beryl. "Sid, you should have seen your face!"

"Very funny." Sid stared down at the currant bun in his hand. It had one big bite taken out of it. "I don't feel like eating this now."

"Don't be silly. Gobble it up, Sid, then go for a walk. You might see her again."

Beryl finished her bun and said goodbye. She waved from the drapery shop doorway. "Give my love to Mum! Tell her I'm fine."

"Yeah, I will. Bye, Beryl."

Sid finished eating his bun and wiped the stickiness off his hands. He started along the main street. Outside the hotel, he waited. He could see Sarah and her father returning, their horses walking quietly in the wide road.

Mr Thorndon nodded a greeting as he slowed his horse to a halt in front of the hotel.

"Hello again!" Sarah's eyes lit up. "Fancy meeting you twice!" She dismounted. "Dad and I are seeing somebody in the hotel. He'll be a while, but I'll be right back." She started tying Talley's reins to the rail in front of the hotel.

"I'll hold her for you," said Sid.

"All right. Thanks, Sid. I'll only be a minute or two."

Sid took the reins and watched as Sarah straightened her hat. He saw out of the corner of his eye that her father was also dismounting.

Mr Thorndon tied his horse's reins to the rail. "Hello again, Sidney," he said. "Come along, Sarah."

"Dad's horse is called Rosie," said Sarah.

"Rosie and Talley." Sid smiled.

As father and daughter disappeared together into the hotel lobby, Sid stroked Talley's soft nose. "Hello, Talley. You're a lovely girl." The pony's coat shone golden as she stood quietly in the morning sun.

"Everett!" A harsh voice startled him. Roger Dyson's face was right in front of him. "Holding a horse again? You love to stand around holding people's horses, don't you?"

Sid glared. "Don't try any of your tricks around this pony, Dyson."

"I don't know what you mean, Everett. I know this pony." Roger stepped closer to Sid. "She's Sarah's." Talley bent her head, and her whiskers brushed the back of Roger's neck. He flung up an elbow and hit the pony in the nose. She pulled back, trying to wheel around at the end of her rein.

Sid moved with her, struggling to calm her. "That's no way to treat a pony."

"She's just retarded," said Roger.

"That's what you said about the captain's horse." Sid stroked the agitated pony's neck.

Sarah appeared on the hotel veranda. "Talley!" she called.

Just then, a passing car backfired, as loud as a gunshot, right next to them. Sid and Roger both jumped. Talley jumped too, jerking the reins free of Sid's grasp. She gave a frightened neigh, showed the whites of her eyes and wheeled around in the road. The car continued on up the street, still backfiring, with Talley taking off in the opposite direction.

Chapter Sixteen

Turnaround

"Talley!" Sid stared wildly up the road.

"You idiot," said Roger, "you let her go."

"The noise frightened her!" Sid rushed to Mr Thorndon's horse and untied her. He leaped up into the saddle. Gritting his teeth, he kicked his heels against the mare's sides. "C'mon, Rosie, let's go!"

Sarah's pony was already a block away, cantering down the middle of the street. People shouted and scattered, and cars pulled out of her way. Sid pursued her, bent over Rosie's neck, his eyes on the fleeing pony. "Come on, girl!" Rosie's hooves pounded on the tarseal, faster and faster, catching up with the pony, until they were side by side.

"Talley! Hey, girl, easy! Talley, hey, it's me, Sid. Talley! Easy, girl." Talley's pace didn't slow. Sid reached out an arm. The horses were neck and neck, but the gap between them was too wide. Sid edged Rosie closer and grabbed for Talley's flapping reins.

Straining, his fingers touched leather. He grabbed at the reins again, caught them and held on tight. Both horses' hooves were thundering on the road. He glimpsed the ground flying beneath him and pulled his eyes away from the stones.

"Talley, good girl," he murmured. "Talley, easy!" Carefully reining in Mr Thorndon's horse, he began to slow the pace.

Sid kept talking as he slowed the horses. He reached out and touched the sweat-soaked neck of the runaway pony. The fear and energy in her body were almost electric. He could hear his own voice, calm, like it was somebody else's, a soothing murmur. In the background, the shouts of the gathering crowd reached his ears. As they slowed to a walk, Sid heard running footsteps behind him. He turned in the saddle. Dad! It was his dad, running towards him. What was Dad doing here in town?

"Sidney." Dad was panting. "I was at the other end of the street. Here, I'll lead the pony." Dad moved to Talley's side and gently stroked her neck. "All right. Calm down now. You're all right. Come on, you little beauty. Let's go back, shall we?" He led her around in a circle, and turned her back towards town.

Sid turned Rosie, and they walked the horses back along the main street together. He could sense people staring, but he kept his gaze straight ahead. His mind was whirling. His dad had calmed the pony in an instant. And now, here he was walking beside him, leading her along the road.

He looked at his father. "Thanks, Dad."

"Just happened to be passing, Sid." Dad cleared his throat. "That was a good bit of rescue work you did there."

Sid swallowed. Suddenly, it was difficult to talk.

Outside the hotel, a crowd was waiting. Sid scanned the faces. There was no sign of Roger.

In front of the hotel, Sid and his dad dismounted.

Mr Thorndon strode up to Sid. His face was grim. "What's going on here? I came out of the hotel—no sign of either of our horses."

"Um..." Sid was unsure of how to answer.

Mr Thorndon said, "Everyone was shouting. I looked up the road, and the Wild West was happening." He raised his eyebrows and waited.

"I was holding Talley, Mr Thorndon, and a car backfired."

"A car backfired?"

"Yes," said Sid. "It gave her a huge fright."

Mr Thorndon frowned.

Sid hesitated. "I tried to hold on to her."

Mr Thorndon gave Sid a hard look. "She's pretty bomb-proof."

"Yes, sir. I know. But it was very sudden. And it was very loud," he added lamely.

Sarah burst in. "Dad, I heard it. She was terrified. It was just like a gun." She glanced at Sid. "And she already seemed to be upset."

Sid offered Rosie's reins to Mr Thorndon. "Your horse, sir."

"Thank you, Sidney." Mr Thorndon took the reins.

Around them, the crowd began to disperse.

Mr Thorndon looked at Sid appraisingly. "An impressive piece of riding, Sidney. Very impressive. You know..." He cleared his throat. "I'm getting ready to hire a new apprentice. The word's been out that your family is moving, so I wasn't sure if you..." he eyed Sid's dad. "Would you all be moving, Arthur, or...?

Sid's eyes locked onto his dad's face. He could see emotions flicker over it.

Dad stayed silent for ages, and then he spoke. "My boy has been wanting something like this for a long time, Mr Thorndon. It would be the thing he would want most, in all the world, I should think."

Sid's eyes widened.

Mr Thorndon nodded. "So, you'd be willing to let your boy stay behind?"

Dad turned his head away. Sid's heart froze. Surely Dad wouldn't go into one of his moods right now, in front of Mr Thorndon? Then Dad turned back. "He deserves his chance, Mr Thorndon. History doesn't always repeat itself."

"Well, Arthur," said Mr Thorndon, "I'll tell you what I'm offering." He glanced at Sid, then turned back to Dad. "Full training. Full board, and two and six a week for himself, which gets put into the bank for him. He doesn't get the money until he's finished his term. There's one condition, and I'm sure you'll agree." He shot a question at Sid, making him jump. "How old are you, Sidney?"

"Fourteen, Mr Thorndon. Almost fifteen. My birthday's really soon."

Mr Thorndon nodded again and turned back to Dad. "He needs to finish school. I'm sure you and Mary would want that."

"Yes, we would," said Dad.

"So, he stays at school until he's fifteen," said Mr Thorndon. "Then he can leave, and no one can stop him. And we'll start his training." He raised his eyebrows. "How does that sound?"

Sid felt his face go hot. It sounded amazing. Like a dream come true. He didn't dare look at his dad's face.

"Sounds pretty good to me," said Dad.

Sid dared to look. Dad was nodding slowly. Sid could tell that Dad thought it was more than good. He thought it was great, but he wasn't going to show it. His father coughed and cleared his throat. "What do you think, Sidney?"

Sid blinked. A shock ran through him. Dad never asked his opinion about anything.

"That sounds really good to me, Mr Thorndon," he said. He hardly dared to breathe as he waited for what his dad would say next.

A long silence hung in the road between them, then Dad spoke. "Well... I think it would be a good thing. Yes. Yes, all right, he can do it."

Sid felt like leaping in the air shouting YES! but he contained himself. Just. His heart was beating so fast he thought everyone would hear it.

"That's agreed then, Arthur," said Mr Thorndon.

Sid watched the men shake hands.

Mr Thorndon turned to him. "Sidney?"

"Yes, sir?"

"You can come and see me. I'll show you around the stables, introduce you to everyone, and show you where you'll sleep."

"Yes, sir. Thank you very much." Sid swallowed down his sense of guilt.

"Not at all, Sidney," said Mr Thorndon.

***

At home, Sid put Hugh back in his paddock and went to find the twins. They were in the barn. "Guess what?"

"What?" they asked.

"I'm not going to Auckland."

They stared at him. "How come?"

"I'm moving to the Thorndon's," said Sid. "Dad agreed I can have an apprenticeship."

"No!"

"It's true," said Sid.

"Where's Dad?" asked Bill.

"He's in town. I saw him in town. And Mr Thorndon. And it's all agreed."

"So, you won't be coming to Auckland with us?" Bruce was squinting at him, his head on one side.

"No. I'll board next door," said Sid. "Like a proper apprentice."

"After all." Bill understood best.

"Yeah, Bill. After all."

"So, no more night riding?" Bill asked.

"I think I'll do one more ride," said Sid. "To celebrate."

"You haven't ridden since your accident." Bill's face twisted up.

"I'm fine, now," said Sid.

"You don't need to do it, Sid," said Bill. "You've got what you wanted."

"Yeah, I know. But it's like a victory lap," said Sid. "It's a celebration."

"Booooys!" Their mother's voice called from the house. "Can you come in? Right now?" Her voice sounded strange. All three boys stared at each other and ran.

The kitchen was dim and golden in the late afternoon light. Dad sat at the table, holding a letter. Mum stood behind him, her hand on his shoulder, Ruby on her hip.

"What is it?" Sid felt a chill rising, filling his insides with ice as he studied his father's face. All the joy and pride that he'd seen there in the street had disappeared. "What's happened?"

"The mill job." Dad paused to gaze around at their faces. "I just got a letter. There's no job anymore."

"What do you mean, Dad?" Sid's voice came out all croaky.

"I mean that there's no job. Literally, no job. The mill burned down. There's no mill any more. So—no mill, no job. No jobs for anyone."

Dad was so still, he seemed carved out of wood.

"So... we aren't going to Auckland?" Bruce's voice squeaked. He cleared his throat and waited, his face looking all thin and pinched, like it did when he was frightened. "Not going?"

"No, Bruce." Mum's voice was quiet. "We're staying here, after all." She smiled a tired smile and brushed her hair back from her face. "Just like normal."

"Dad?" It was Bill. "There might be other jobs in Auckland."

Dad slammed his hand on the table, and they all jumped. "Yes, I'm sure there are. But I'm here and the jobs are there. And I don't know if I'd get any other job in Auckland. I was just lucky with the mill job. I thought. And now there'll be a whole lot more men up there looking for jobs. All the ones from that mill - they'll join the job queue." He sighed. "I'll stay here. Keep hoeing turnips."

They all noticed it at once. The sound of a car engine outside. All heads turned. Cars never came here. But the engine was getting louder. There was a car, and it was coming up the driveway.

Dad, already on his feet, went to the door.

The engine stopped and there was the sound of car doors opening and closing.

Dad spoke. "Hello? Can I help you?"

Sid crowded in the doorway with his brothers, peering around Dad. A man and a woman stood there, smartly dressed.

"Mr Everett?" said the man.

"Yes," said Dad.

"Jim Baldwin, from the Ministry of Education."

Sid heard Mum gasp behind him.

"I'd like to talk to Mrs Everett, if I may," said Mr Baldwin. "If she's at home."

"You'd better come in," said Dad.

He stepped back, and Sid and his brothers hurried out of the way. The two strangers entered. Mum's eyes were bright, and her cheeks were flushed. She still had Ruby on her hip, and she looked as though she'd fight anyone who tried to lay a hand on her.

"How do you do, Mrs Everett?" said Mr Baldwin.

"How do you do?" Mum glanced around. "Won't you sit down? Sidney, clear the table."

There was nothing on the table but the letter about the mill. Sid grabbed it and put in on the mantelpiece.

"Please sit down," said Mum.

The lady smiled at Ruby, but she didn't sit down.

The man cleared his throat. "Mrs Everett, I have come to apologise."

Mum blinked.

"Please allow me to explain." The man took a letter from his pocket. "This is a carbon copy of a letter we sent to you some time ago, pointing out that your daughter Ruby ought to be in school. I'm sure you're familiar with its contents."

"Yes," said Mum.

He inclined his head towards Ruby. "Is this Ruby?"

"Yes," said Mum again.

"Very good." He cleared his throat again. "Now. Not long ago, my wife and I were visiting families in this area, whose children have special learning needs. We had intended to visit you as well. But a near accident put us off. We almost ran over a little girl."

Mum stared at him.

"Yes," he said. "I am the guilty party who not only almost ran over a small child, but who berated her mother for allowing her to stray into danger."

Mum's lips twitched into a smile. "I would probably have done the same," she said. "We were all shocked."

The man eyed her sharply, then continued. "But when I realised the girl was one of our own, a deaf child who would come under our care, I was mortified. I was also extremely shaken by what could have occurred. I couldn't continue with my duties that day, but retired with my wife to the hotel where we were staying." He glanced at his wife, then back at Mum. "However," he said, "having recovered my equilibrium, I am here to make you an apology. And not only an apology, but an offer."

"An offer?" said Mum faintly.

"How would you like, Mrs Everett, to go to Auckland, to visit the school for the deaf in Titirangi, and see for yourself what it's like there?"

"Oh!" said Mum.

"You could meet the teachers," said Mr Baldwin. "See what the children are learning, see where they sleep, and how they are cared for." He paused. "And we would pay all expenses."

"Goodness," Mum said. "The government pays for that?"

"No, actually. My wife and I, out of concern for you and your situation, and out of our genuine regret at the distress we caused you, would like to arrange this."

Mum's eyes were bright. "Arthur?"

"Go." Dad raised his chin. "Go and see, Mary. It's a good offer."

Mum turned to the man and inclined her head. "Thank you." She hesitated. "I'll need a bit of time to think about it. But I'm very grateful for your offer. I'll let you know as soon as I can."

***

In the shadowy bedroom, Sid lay in his bed, listening to his brothers breathing. He studied the patterns made by the moonlight on the wall, tensing himself, ready for a night ride.

"Sid?" It was Bill. He wasn't asleep.

"What?" said Sid.

"You're not going out, are you?"

"Yes, I am," said Sid.

"You don't need to," said Bill. "You've got what you want."

"Yes, I know. But it's like a victory lap. Like I said. It's a celebration. Once more on the beach with Silver. It's a full moon tonight." He slipped out of bed and grabbed his jersey. "What could happen?"

Chapter Seventeen

Last Beach Ride

Sit stepped out from the black shadows into the next-door paddock. He could hear the horses breathing. The moonlight was so bright that he imagined it that warmed him. The horses stood still, watching him.

"Silver," he called softly.

None of the horses moved. They were like shining statues in the silver wash of moonlight.

"Silver!" As he approached, one horse separated itself from the herd.

"Hello, Silver!" Sid rubbed the horse's neck and slipped the bridle over his head. "Haven't seen you for a while, have I? One last ride on the beach, eh, boy?"

He led Silver out into the lane. The still night air carried the distant sound of waves thundering on the beach.

The tide must be full in. I'll have to ride higher on the sand, where it's softer. Have to be careful... Perhaps I shouldn't go?

He shook the thoughts off. Nah. He was going. He checked that the gate was shut, and swung himself up into the saddle.

When they got to the beach, Silver stopped. He whinnied and shook his head.

"C'mon, boy, what's the matter?" Sid felt strangely hesitant, himself. The sea pounded and washed against the shore. The sand glistened in the moonlight. It seemed like a strange, alien landscape he had visited a long time ago.

It's just that I haven't been here for a while.

But something was different. Sid scanned the beach. He realised it had changed since the storm. The little stream was narrower and deeper. But that wasn't it... Suddenly he realised the log was gone. The massive log, embedded in sand with its branches reaching up at the sky, had seemed unmovable, like it would lie there forever. Now the beach where it had lain was clear and smooth. Only a line of seaweed, left by the tide, interrupted the wide sweep of sand.

"C'mon, Silver," said Sid. "C'mon, boy. It's all right. Nothing to worry about. We've done this heaps of times." Sid pushed his heels into Silver's sides and urged him forward. Silver moved into a trot, then into a canter.

As the sea air rushed into his lungs and the stars wheeled overhead, Sid's heart soared. He laughed aloud. "Go, Silver! Let's have a gallop!"

As they flew along, something white loomed up in the dark-ness ahead - branches clawing at the sky. Sid yelled, pulling on the reins. "Woah, Silver, Woah..."

Too late to swerve, Silver took the jump. Sid crouched low as they soared together, then felt the impact as Silver's leg clipped a branch. A branch that reached up higher than the tree trunk and stretched out like a clawed hand. Silver twisted awkwardly, and Sid flew through the air. His body hit the wet sand like a pig carcass thrown into a truck.

All of his breath knocked out of him, he lay stunned, pain shooting through his body. His mouth was full of sand, and his ears were full of the sound of Silver, snorting and struggling to his feet.

Gasping, his head spinning, Sid crawled over to where Silver stood. He tried to keep his voice steady, but horror filled him as he touched sticky blood on the horse's leg, and felt him trembling.

"All right, Silver. It's going to be all right."

In the moonlight, Silver's eyes were rolling. Sid felt despair flooding his veins. He peered closer. It was a gash. What should he do? He pulled off his jumper, then his shirt. He ripped the shirt in half, wrapping it firmly around Silver's leg.

His voice shook as he kept on talking. He tried to sound calm. "It's all right, Silver. I'll go for help. You... you..." He couldn't think of what to say. Passing the reins over Silver's head, with shaky fingers, he undid the buckle on one side of the bit. He wrapped the long reins a few times around a sturdy branch. That would have to do.

"Please stand there, Silver, and don't pull on it. You'll have to wait for me." He tied his jumper around his waist and backed away. "I'll go as fast as I can."

Turning away, he began to run. Staggering along the sand, gasping for breath, he stopped only once to look back. Silver stood in the moonlight, beside the white tree.

"I'll be back," he whispered. Then he ran on.

The way seemed endless. How far had they ridden? Where was the road back to the farm? He scanned the sand dunes. Now that the log had moved, he had no landmark to show him the way. Panic engulfed him, then in a moment of clarity, he remembered he could track their course by the hoof prints in the sand. He looked down. There they were, velvet-black prints, showing the way. He followed them, reached the small stream, and splashed through it.

Stumbling up and over the dunes, panting and clutching at handfuls of slippery dune grasses to stop himself from sliding, he finally reached the short, scrubby grassland next to the road.

His lungs burning, his mind full of Silver and his pain, he ran on. His boots crunched on the gravel. Moonlight and shadow flickered across his path. Fear and horror, like living things close behind him, pursued him along the dark, winding lane.

What if Silver died? How could he live with it? And how could he tell Mr Thorndon what he'd done?

Chapter Eighteen

Despair

Sid stopped for a minute on the road, gasping, doubled over. He had to think.

Should I run straight to Mr Thorndon? Or home to Dad? Home's nearer. It would be quicker to wake Dad. But Mr Thorndon could ride down on another horse. That would be the quickest.

Nevertheless, Sid found his footsteps taking him towards home.

Jess met him at the door, wagging her tail. In the house, the ticking clock filled the silence. Moonlight streamed around him, painting his shadow black on the floor. Sid crashed the door back against the wall. He wanted to wake everybody. Who cared, now, what they thought? Silver was down on the beach, alone... He started along the dark hallway towards his parents' bedroom.

"Dad!" Sid shook his father. "Dad, wake up!"

In a few words, he told his father what had happened and where Silver was. Dad didn't hesitate. He started pulling on his clothes.

"I'll get down there right now," said Dad. "You go up to the Thorndon's. Wake them up and tell them what's happened.

They'll have bandages and ointment, and they can get there quickly on horseback." He glanced at the alarm clock next to the bed. "It will take them a bit of time to find all that stuff and saddle up a horse. If I go down to the beach now, on foot, I'll probably get there first." He turned to his wife. "Mary? I'll need something for bandages."

Mum was out of bed, pulling her dressing gown around herself. "I'll find an old sheet," she said. "Sidney, you need to wear something warm." She hurried out of the room without waiting for an answer.

Sid sat on the edge of his parents' bed, feeling sick. Would Silver have to be put down because of him? Or be forever lame? The linen cupboard door closed with a squeak, and Mum returned with a sheet in her hands.

"Thank you." Dad turned to Sid. "I'll do what I can for the horse, Sid, and I'll wait for you and Mr Thorndon." He grabbed a torch. "At the beach, do I go left or right?"

"Right," said Sid.

"You sure?"

Sid nodded.

"Alright," said Dad. His eyes met Sid's. His gaze was alert, full of confidence. "Don't worry, Sid. We'll do the best we can. You and me. That's all anyone can do when it comes down to it."

Sid felt calmer. His dad seemed to have understood every-thing, and to have taken charge. He didn't even seem angry.

"Alright," said Dad. "Go now!"

Sid ran.

***

Running to the Thorndon's, Sid's breath came in big gasps. There was a roaring noise in his ears, and his legs felt heavy, like they belonged to somebody else and he couldn't control them properly. He felt sick. Despair gripped him again as he remembered Silver standing alone on the sand, and the sticky texture of blood. He reached the Thorndon's gate, gleaming white in the moonlight, and bent over, retching into the long grass.

Steeling himself, he continued running, his boots crunching on the gravel driveway. As he wound through the trees, the flickering moonlight between the branches was dizzying, making everything feel unreal. Then he came out into the wide, open space in front of the house. He realised his cheeks were wet.

Tears. Well, who cares?

He banged on the door.

****

"Mr Thorndon," Sid gasped, his heart hammering so hard and his breathing so strained from all the running that he struggled to get the words out. He saw the alarm in Mr Thorndon's eyes.

"Steady, boy," said Mr Thorndon. "What's happened? Is it your dad?"

"No, it's Silver."

"Silver?" said Mr Thorndon.

"Your horse, Mr Thorndon. I was riding him on the beach. He's hurt. I think he's hurt badly..."

Mr Thorndon didn't wait to hear any more. Pulling on a heavy coat over his pyjamas, he told Sid gruffly to sit down. "Get your breath back, boy, and pull yourself together. I'll get my horse and we'll go down there right away." He disappeared out into the darkness.

Sid stood and shivered. He pulled his jumper on, but he was still shivering when Mr Thorndon returned, leading Rosie. He was also holding a hooded jacket.

"Here, put this on. Then I'm going to tie some blankets across your back."

Sid struggled into the jacket, then stood still while Mr Thorndon secured the horse blankets.

Mr Thorndon hesitated. "I suppose I'd better take a gun. Just in case."

Sid's heart froze. "Mr Thorndon?"

"Yes?"

"My dad's with him."

"Your dad?" said Mr Thorndon. "Was he on the beach with you?"

"No. I went to him first…" Sid looked around helplessly. "He's gone to be with Silver. He'll do what he can." He stared wildly at Mr Thorndon. "Please hurry!"

Mr Thorndon went into the house, then reappeared with a rifle. "Alright, boy. You can jump up behind me." He mounted his horse and reached down to help Sid up. "Let's go."

Sid jolted along, mounted behind Mr Thorndon. His neck itched where it rubbed against the heavy woollen blankets that Mr Thorndon had tied across his back. He clung to the sturdy figure in front, his cheek pressed against the roughness of Mr Thorndon's coat, breathing in the smell of warm horse and woollen cloth. Again, the moonlight flickered between black tree branches as they rode, making everything seem as if it were moving in rapid jerks of black and silver. Sid felt as though he was an actor in a film, or that it was all a dream. His eyelids grew heavy.

***

As they came out onto the wide sweep of sand, Sid opened his eyes. The memory of tonight's disaster hit his stomach, lurching him back to reality. How could he have fallen asleep? The tide was going out, and Sid could hear the surf's heavy roll, somewhere out in the darkness. The sand shone wet in the moonlight, and the trails of Silver's hoof prints and his own returning footprints were clearly visible.

"They're further along, Mr Thorndon," he said.

Mr Thorndon grunted. Turning his horse into the wind, he followed the prints up the glittering beach to where a dark shape stood beneath stark white branches stretched towards the moon.

As they reached the scene, Sid's heart began pounding in his chest. "Mr Thorndon can probably feel it," he thought, "through his coat." He sat upright, pulling himself away from the warmth of the broad back. At once, he began shivering.

"You can dismount, boy." Mr Thorndon waited until Sid got his cold-stiffened legs over the horse and down onto the ground, then he dismounted, too. He peered into the darkness beneath the white branches. "Arthur. How is he?"

Sid saw his dad's face, a pale shape in the shadows, raised to answer. "He seems to be all right, Mr Thorndon. Can't see much."

"Hang on, I've got a lantern." Mr Thorndon tied Rosie to one of the gleaming branches of the dead tree. Sid heard him rummaging in his satchel, then he bought out a small kerosene lantern and squatted down on the sand. There was the sharp strike of a match. Shielding it from the wind with his body, Mr Thorndon lit the lantern, then stood up. "This'll shed a bit of light on things."

The lantern flared, throwing Dad and Silver into sharp detail and making the beach behind them disappear into inky blackness.

"It's his leg," said Dad. "Sid bandaged it, but I took that off, and I've tied a fresh bandage on the wound." He paused. "It's a gash. Feels like quite a big one."

Sid watched the faces of the two men, lit by the yellow glow. His dad's face was bony, his eyes bright and alert. Mr Thorndon's face was broad and frowning. The difference in his father struck Sid again—he seemed like a new man. It was as if the emergency had brought out the best in him. He was brave and resourceful and quick thinking. And above all, as steady as a rock. He remembered Jack's words.

He's a hero, Sid. He's a man you can trust with your life, no matter what. Don't you worry about your father, Sid. He'll come right.

Sid tried to control his shivering. He leaned over to watch Mr Thorndon's experienced hands run down the horse's foreleg, feeling for breaks. Silver stood quietly, his head drooping. Mr Thorndon's hands reached the bandages made from the sheet that Dad had ripped up. Sid looked away. He gazed up at Silver's face, just above the two men's heads. He could see marks on his neck where the sweat had dried.

Silver's eye rolled as Mr Thorndon's hands moved over his foreleg.

"Silver." Sid spoke gently. "Silver, it's me, Sid."

Chapter Nineteen

Silver Lining

Mr Thorndon's hands hesitated when they reached the bandage on Silver's leg, then they moved on.

"I'll leave that for the moment," he said. "Nicely done, Arthur." He glanced up at Sid's dad. "Just the ticket. We'll not touch it yet." He looked at Sid. "Can you put a couple of blankets over him?"

Sid was shivering so hard that his whole body shook and his teeth were chattering. He could hardly control his hands as he unrolled one of the horse blankets, fighting the wind to keep it from tangling.

"Silver!" He spoke gently. The horse lifted his head. Sid's gut twisted with fear and remorse. "Here's a blanket for you, boy."

"That's good, Sidney." Mr Thorndon's voice was a rumble from down near Silver's leg. "You talk to him, keep him calm."

Sid glanced at his dad. Dad was looking at him and the corners of his mouth were turned up in a tiny smile. Sid's heart lurched, and he felt warmer all of a sudden. He spread one blanket over Silver and then another.

"Easy, Silver, easy boy..." Sid's voice sounded shaky in his own ears. He reached out a hand and his voice strengthened.

"Good boy, Silver. You'll be all right. We'll look after you. It's okay now..." He smoothed back the dark forelock. "Everything's going to be all right..."

His heart felt sick and he could barely lift his arm - it seemed extremely heavy for some reason. But he kept talking, his voice steady. The horse's eyes were calm, gazing into the distance.

As Sid continued speaking, he stroked the soft neck, wondering all the time if what he was saying was only a lot of empty words, used to placate a doomed horse. The horse he loved, but had risked, for the sake of a crazy gallop.

All that matters is to keep calm and to make every moment feel safe for Silver. Even if they do turn out to be his last moments of life.

Finally, Mr Thorndon stood up and stepped back. Sid searched his face anxiously. He saw Mr Thorndon's eyes stray to the rifle that stood propped against the dead tree, its barrel gleaming in the moonlight. His stomach lurched, but then he saw Mr Thorndon's eyes meet his dad's, saw the faint shake of his head and the fleeting smile. He sensed the current of understanding that passed between the two men.

Mr Thorndon made up his mind. "Arthur, I'm going for the vet. Nothing's broken. I'll bring the horse truck down as far as the beach and we'll get him home. Can you stay with him?"

"Yes, of course," said Dad. He looked at Sid. "Sid and I will stay with him. Won't we, son?" Sid nodded, too overcome by tiredness and emotion to answer.

"It might take me a while. I'll leave you the lantern," said Mr Thorndon. He turned, mounted his horse, and rode back along the beach, leaving them alone with Silver. Sid stood next to Silver with one arm around him, listening to his breathing and the distant roar of surf away out in the darkness.

The world shank until it was just a circle of lantern light containing a man, a boy, and a stricken horse.

"Get some sleep, son." Sid's dad sat down with his back against the log. "There's another blanket here. I'll stay awake."

Sid shot a look at his father. Dad had a calm sort of expression on his face that Sid hadn't seen before. He didn't argue. The night's anguish had left him exhausted. He curled up next to his dad and fell asleep immediately, the rough edge of a horse blanket against his cheek.

***

Sometime later, something woke him. He lifted his head and sat up. The tide had gone a long way out, and the hiss and roar of the waves was dull and distant. The moon had moved, and the sky was no longer clear. Immense clouds like glowing white mountains drifted across the sky. He looked over at Silver. The horse was standing quietly, breathing steadily in the darkness. Sid felt warm and lightheaded. He sensed the bulk of his dad's tall, bony frame next to him.

He struggled into a more upright position, so that he could see his dad's face. Dad was gazing into the darkness, his hard features softened by the lantern light. He had a far-away look on his face, as though he had discovered something, or saw something really wonderful, something Sid couldn't see.

"Dad?" said Sid.

"You awake, son?"

"Yes." Sid paused. "What are you thinking about?"

"You, my boy." Dad glanced down at him. "I've been thinking about you. Wanting to be a jockey. Isn't that what this is all about? Sneaking off and riding on the beach. I have to hand it to you, you've got determination. And I've been thinking, if I had a bit of that kind of determination myself, it might make all the difference. For me and Mother. Turn our lives around."

"It wasn't such a great idea, as it turns out," said Sid.

"Yes, well..." Dad's voice was gruff. "I'm just sorry I didn't listen to you, when I should have. But you've taught me a lesson. And there's nothing like a midnight drama to wake a man up to what's important."

He smiled, and Sid felt a warm glow deep inside.

"You snuggle down again, Sidney," Dad said. "Get some sleep while you can. I'll go on thinking about things. It'll take Mr Thorndon a while to get hold of the vet and bring him down here. We might not see him until the morning."

Sid pulled the horse blanket around himself and lay down again, curled up against his dad. The last thing he heard, before dropping back into dreamlessness, was the sound of his father playing the harmonica. He imagined the soft notes of We'll Meet Again floating like musical sparks into the black sky.

Chapter Twenty

Explanations

Sid woke again. He was lying slumped against his dad, and he could hear his heavy breathing. He forced his eyes open and had a close view of fine grains of gold and silver. A dusting of sand covered his tongue as he licked his lips. His cheek was resting on the cold sand, and the smell of brine and seaweed filled his nostrils. His back ached. It was very dark, as the moon had set, but Sid sensed morning approaching. He groaned as images came flooding back—the night ride, the dead tree, the horse...

"Silver!" He leapt up.

"He's all right, Sid. He's doing all right." Dad's voice sounded tired. "How are you, son?"

"I'm okay." Sid peered over at Silver, still standing.

"I've been checking on him," said Dad. "He's all right. But I'll be glad to see the vet arrive."

The vet. Sid's insides turned to ice. He squatted down again, next to his father. He felt his dad put the blanket back around his shoulders.

"Is it nearly morning, Dad?" he asked.

"It's getting towards morning, son," said Dad. "The wind's changing and the sky's getting lighter. Mr Thorndon should be here soon."

Sid's heart sank at the mention of Mr Thorndon. He hunched closer to his dad, sharing his warmth, and tugged the horse blanket around himself as best he could.

"Dad?" Sid waited, but his father didn't answer. "Dad?"

"Yes, son?"

"Dad... I'm so sorry..." he said. "I never thought this would happen. I know it's all my fault. And if Silver has to be put down...." He couldn't finish. He couldn't trust his voice to carry on talking and not crack up into tears.

"Sid," Dad's voice was thoughtful, "it looks like it was your fault, but I'm wondering if it might actually be all my fault."

"Your fault?" Sid croaked out the words. "But Dad, you didn't even know what I was doing!"

"No, I didn't know. But I should have known." Dad paused. "Well, I know now. You've been riding down here at night, alone. Nobody guessed what you were up to. And you were riding a valuable horse that didn't belong to you."

Sid cringed inside. Dad had a knack of laying things out in the worst possible light. "I wanted to train. To be a jockey. It's what I've always wanted." He paused. "There didn't seem to be any other way." He could tell it sounded pretty lame, even as he said it.

"When you feel like that, son," said Dad, "it's usually not true. Never believe there's only one option. There's always another way. You just have to find it. Sometimes you need to ask someone."

Sid was silent.

Ask who? Dad? Not likely.

As if he had read his thoughts, his father continued. "You didn't want to talk to me. I understand that. I don't blame you."

Dad cleared his throat again. "I must have been a bit difficult to live with."

Sid couldn't believe his ears. Dad never talked like this. "I talk to Mum, sometimes."

"But not about this," said Dad.

"No," said Sid.

"Sidney," said Dad, "I blame myself. I didn't realise how determined you were, or how much it mattered to you. I was against you being a jockey. I didn't want you to have anything to do with that business."

"Well, I don't think it's going to happen now, anyway." Sid scooped up a handful of sand and threw it down. "Mr Thorndon won't have me now."

"It might be for the best, son. Best not to bother with being a jockey."

"Why, Dad?"

"Why?" asked Dad.

"Yes. Why don't you want me to be a jockey?"

Dad didn't answer straight away. Sid waited, listening to the hiss and roar of the waves. He glanced up at his father's face. Suddenly, he wasn't sure that he wanted to hear the answer to his question.

"Well…" Dad's voice was reluctant. "I saw a nasty accident a long time ago. And I saw the cheating that goes on, or can sometimes go on, in the racing world. I quit then and went and worked on a road gang."

"You quit?" said Sid. "What do you mean, quit?"

"I was a jockey, Sid, when I was young. Before I met your mother."

"You were a jockey?" Sid was stunned. "I never knew that."

"Yup," said Dad. "I was a jockey. For a while."

"You never told us," said Sid.

"It goes back a long way, Sidney. Before you were born. When I was your age, I was dead keen to be a jockey, just like you."

"And you quit," said Sid. "So... what happened?"

"Do you understand what it means to 'throw a race'?" asked Dad.

"Yes, it means you lose on purpose."

"That's right." Dad's voice got a bitter edge to it. "You don't lose on purpose so much as you just don't ride to win. It's wrong. It's dishonest. And it's not racing. There's no joy in it."

"Did you throw a race?"

"I was told to throw a race. I didn't want to do it, and I decided I would ride to win. So, I rode to win. I was riding a jumper, Sid. A beautiful jumper. 'Avon', his name was. Anyway, I rode him to win, and we hit a jump and fell. Avon was put down because he was badly injured. And I was in trouble, for riding hard and for losing a valuable horse."

Shock waves ran through Sid as he listened. He had never imagined that his dad had any real knowledge of racing. And here he was, he had actually been a jockey. Sid felt a pang of pity for the boy his dad had been, determined not to do wrong.

"So, what happened then?" he asked.

"They were pretty angry with me," said Dad. "They left me alone for a while. Just let me ride. Some of my races I won. I was happy. I loved horses, and I loved racing. Then they wanted me to throw another race." Dad paused. "Funny how it all comes back. Seems like yesterday. Well, I rode like I didn't care, because I didn't care. What's the point, if you can't ride to win? I came in somewhere near the back. And when I got off that horse, I walked out of the stables and never went back. Never picked up my wages or anything."

Sid was quiet, picturing the boy who was now his dad, walking away from racing, never to return.

"So that's why you didn't want me training to race?" he asked.

"Yes, that's why," said Dad. "I didn't find it easy, those outings to the races with the Cunninghams. You remember? When you were a little boy?"

"I remember," said Sid.

"When I saw you'd set your heart on being a jockey, I stopped us going. I thought you'd grow out of it. But you never did." Dad paused. "It's in the blood, I suppose." Dad got to his feet and walked over to Silver. He stroked the horse's neck, and looked back at Sid. "I can't stop you, Sidney. You'll do what you want to do. Just go in with your eyes open, that's all. It's not all glory."

Sid sat hunched up, listening to the crash and boom of the waves, and watching his father with Silver in the growing light. He watched his father's hand stroking the horse. A gentle hand. A hand that understood horses. He thought about all those years his father had kept his jockey days a secret. He felt like something had broken, but something else had mended in his heart.

He got up and joined his dad. "Good morning, Silver," he said. He reached up and cupped his hand under the soft muzzle. His eyes lingered on the bandaged leg. Silver nickered softly. The pale light of morning was creeping onto the beach, giving a dull colour to everything that the darkness had hidden.

Dad stepped away and lit a cigarette, the glow of the match briefly illuminating his face. Sid watched him walk down to where the sea foam hissed onto the sand. He stood there for a moment, then he turned and came back. Sid gave a start. His dad's face was shining. His face shone with an inner strength—as if he'd won a great victory.

"They're here." Dad's voice cut through his thoughts. "Mr Thorndon and the vet. They must have the horse truck waiting in the lane. It's time to deal with the music, lad."

Sid turned around and his heart froze. He almost staggered—the sudden clutch of fear and dismay was so overwhelming.

"Dad?"

"Yes, Sid?"

"He's going to be so mad."

"Sid, we don't know yet how it'll turn out," Dad said. "And I'm here."

"Yeah, you're here." A glow of gratitude took Sid by surprise. "Thanks, Dad."

In the growing light of morning, Sid could see figures approaching on foot along the sand. Mr Thorndon, of course, and the shorter one must be the vet. But there was a third figure. He caught a flash of blonde hair and a bolt of dismay ran through him.

Sarah! Oh no, he's brought Sarah with him!

Chapter Twenty-One

The Vet and the Verdict

Mr Thorndon got there first. "Morning, Arthur. How's Silver doing?"

"He's holding up," said Dad.

Sid dared, once, to look at Sarah. Her eyes, when they met his, made him cringe inside. He knew she was here because she cared about Silver. He was pretty sure that she was also here to let him know what she thought of him.

The vet nodded a greeting and knelt beside Silver. Sid was aware that Mr Thorndon and Sarah were standing next to his dad. They watched as the vet began his examination, running gentle hands over Silver's leg. The vet opened his bag. As he began to untie the bandage, Sid had to look away.

No one spoke to him, but Sid felt their blame. He was the fool, the deceiver, the destroyer. Never to be trusted again. He turned and stumbled away up the beach.

From a distance, he watched, wondering what was happening. He had hated standing there by the horse, feeling everyone despising him, but this was worse. He had to know. He jogged back.

Dad smiled as he arrived next to him. "He's going to be all right, Sidney."

"Really?" said Sid.

"Incredibly lucky!" The vet raised an eyebrow. "Could've been much worse. I've stitched him up and given him something for the pain. Given him a tetanus shot, too. New thing. They used it in the war." He glanced at Dad.

"That's right," Dad said.

The vet snapped his bag shut.

"All right, Mr Thorndon. Let's get this horse of yours into the truck."

Sid followed the halting march back along the beach. He ached to walk alongside Silver, to talk to him, to help him make it to the horse truck. But he didn't dare. His place was at the back.

Mr Thorndon led Silver into the darkness of the horse truck and secured him. Then he closed the door. He looked at Sid, opened his mouth as if to say something, then shut it again. He turned to Sid's dad. "Thanks very much, Arthur. Can we give you a lift back?"

"I'd appreciate it, Mr Thorndon, if you've got room."

Sid slumped into the back seat next to his dad. It was the most miserable ride of his life. It wasn't far, but it seemed endless. His mind ran between two torments—wondering how Silver was and wondering what Sarah was thinking. She sat in the front seat next to her father, her head high.

When Sid climbed stiffly out at the gate, he risked a glance at her. She looked back at him, her eyes narrowed. Then she turned her face away.

Chapter Twenty-Two

Crazy Jack

On the morning of his fifteenth birthday, Sid woke early. Sparrows were chirping in the eaves above his window and magpies warbled far off in the distance. A shaft of early sunlight shone in through a gap in the curtains, lighting up the faded green and gold wallpaper. He twitched aside a corner of the curtain. The sun was just touching the tops of the distant hills. He slipped out of bed and tiptoed to the bathroom to wash his face and comb his hair. The he dressed carefully and crept out of the house and over to the barn.

Sid tried not to think too hard as he climbed the ladder through the dusty darkness and up into the loft where his tin of newspaper cuttings was hidden. He'd made up his mind. This was the end of the dream. He pulled aside the wooden boards and there was the tin, gleaming softly in the early light. He tucked it under his arm and climbed back down the ladder.

In the kitchen he opened the small door in the front of the coal range, making a light dusting of ash fall onto the hearth, and prised the lid off the tin.

Don't think about it.

The firebox was cold, with a thin layer of pinkish-brown ash from last night's fire. He stuffed in handfuls of cuttings.

Just a bit of old newsprint. That's all.

When the tin was empty he struck a match and set the newspaper cuttings alight. Dry and crisp, they burst into flame, warming his face as he watched them burn. He watched until they were nothing but a pile of black fragments, still glowing with golden sparks and making tiny tinkling sounds as they cooled. It had taken less than a minute.

He put the big, round tin on the kitchen bench, a small smile twitching his lips.

Mum'll be surprised to see that again.

He went outside and saddled Hugh, then he rode to town, wearing the one good shirt and pair of trousers that he owned.

***

At the picnic grounds, he tied Hugh to the railing. A man was sleeping on a park bench. Sid studied him. Something about the man was familiar. There was a big bundle sticking out from under the bench. As he watched, the man lifted his head and gazed around.

"Hey, Jack!" Sid waved. "How are you doing?"

Jack sat up and stared, not answering.

Sid walked over. "Tell your wife her dream was spot on."

"What?" said Jack.

"Her dream," said Sid. "About my dad. The matakite thing."

Jack stood up. He reached under the bench and hauled out the bundle. "I dunno who you are, but you can just leave me alone," he said.

Sid blinked. "It's me, Jack. Sid Everett. Arthur Everett's son."

"Don't remember you. Don't know any Arthur. Move out of my way, boy."

Jack pushed past, roughly, and headed towards the town.

Sid watched him go, feeling uneasy. Jack was definitely getting stranger. Then he shrugged and followed. He might as well be first in line at the job office. Maybe he couldn't have his dream, but he was going to make sure that Beryl achieved hers.

In the employment office, a typewriter clattered somewhere out of sight, and voices hummed in a far-off room. A man behind a desk beckoned him over. He was wearing a white shirt and a tie.

"Have a seat, son," said the man.

There was a wooden chair in front of the desk. Sid sat down.

The employment officer picked up a fountain pen and removed the cap. He poised the nib over a printed form. "May I have your name?"

Sid cleared his throat. "Sidney John Everett." He watched as his name was entered on the form in fine, flowing handwriting.

"Date of birth?"

"Fourteenth of October, 1931."

"Birthday today, eh?"

"Yup," said Sid.

The man studied him. "Fifteen years old. What kind of work are you looking for, son? Not that there's a lot of choice."

Sid shrugged. "Anything. Work on the roads. I don't mind what I do."

"Hmmm," said the man. "You're a bit skinny for most of the work we could give you. It is mostly on the roads." The man narrowed his eyes appraisingly. "You look kind of like a jockey, to me. Probably never going to be big. Ever thought about it?"

Sid stared. "Once," he said.

"You're built for it," said the man.

"No," said Sid.

"All right. Got no jockey jobs, anyway. You need an apprenticeship for that. We can put you on a road gang, straight away. Plenty of work on the roads. If you think you're up to it."

"That'll do," said Sid.

The man handed him the sheet of paper and placed his pen next to it. "Here you are then. Have a read of this. If it suits you, sign on the dotted line."

Sid sat for a while, looking at the paper, not reading the words. Then he picked up the pen, and wrote his name, Sidney Everett, in clear schoolboy script.

***

"So, you've done it?" Beryl widened her eyes. "Truly?"

"Yup," said Sid. "Signed up. I'm a working man. And you're going back to school. You're going to sit your exams, and you're going to be a teacher."

Beryl glanced around, but Mrs Archibald was nowhere in sight. "I think she's in the office. But keep your voice down," she said. "Wow, Sid, I can't believe it! You shouldn't have done that. I'll be fine."

"No," said Sid. "You'll do what you've always wanted to do. I'll make sure of it."

"What about your dream?" Beryl asked. "Being a jockey?"

"What about yours?" Sid waved a pair of gloves under Beryl's nose. "This isn't your dream, either."

"I get my wages." Beryl frowned at Sid. "You didn't have to quit trying to be a jockey. You shouldn't have. I didn't think you'd give up that easily."

"Easily? Do you think I've given up easily?" Sid slammed the gloves down on the counter. "I don't expect Mr Thorndon will give me another chance. And Sarah..."

"Sarah probably needs a bit of time." Beryl smoothed out the gloves.

"She hates me," said Sid. "You should have seen her face. She looked at me like I was a piece of dirt."

Beryl changed the subject. "What did they say to you, at the labour exchange?"

"Oh," said Sid, "they asked if I'd ever considered being a jockey."

"You're joking!" said Beryl. "Did they have a jockey job for you?"

"Of course not," said Sid. "He just said I looked like a jockey." Sid grimaced. "Mum once told me I never like to give up much. She was right, I don't. But sometimes, you have to. And it's for a good cause. The 'Beryl Becomes a Teacher' cause. I'm backing your dream now." He paused. Beryl was looking past him, over his shoulder.

"Something's happening in the street, Sid," she said.

He spun around. Through the shop window, he could see people running. A crowd was gathering in front of the Position Office. He felt a sickening premonition of danger. "Stay here, Beryl. I'm going to see what's happening."

Sid joined the crowd, standing on tiptoe to see past heads and over shoulders. He could hear whispers, but most people were silent, all staring at something. With a shock, he recognised the key players in a small, horrifying drama. On the steps of the Post Office stood Jack, with a rifle. The rifle was pointed at a short, older man in a grey suit. It was Major Thorndon, Sarah's grandfather. With an even greater shock, he saw his dad, moving carefully, stepping out from the crowd.

"Jack," said Dad, "it's me, Arthur."

"I don't know you," growled Jack.

"You do know me, Jack," said Dad. "It's your old mate, Arthur, and you know me well. We signed up together. We served together. First echelon." He took another step nearer. "Closer than brothers. Saved each other's lives, more than once. You know me, Jack."

Jack stared, then nodded. "I know you, Arthur," he said.

"That's good. That's very good," said Dad. "Now give me the gun, Jack."

Jack didn't reply, but his knuckles whitened as he gripped the rifle tighter.

Sarah's grandfather stood very still, facing the rifle. His eyes were on Jack's. He didn't look scared. He was keeping calm and letting Dad do the talking.

Dad took another step. "Time to go home, mate," he said. Jack was silent, his face tense with concentration.

Dad spoke again. "Can I have the gun, Jack?"

"Get out of here, Arthur," said Jack. "Hurry, and I'll cover you. I've got this fella cornered."

"Jack," said Dad, "he's not the enemy. He's a friend. He's one of ours."

"Not on your life, he isn't," said Jack. "Get away, Arthur, while you can. I owe you one, and this is it."

"No." Dad didn't take his eyes off Jack. "Jack, your wife's here."

Again, Jack didn't answer. The silence lengthened and thickened until Sid felt that he could hardly breathe.

"She's waiting to take you home," said Dad.

Sid scanned the crowd. There she was, her sons Peter and James next to her. They looked ready to spring. He wondered if they would.

Mr Thorndon was there too, standing like a bear ready to swipe, not moving. Old Captain Findlay was there. His eyes glittered as they flicked from Jack to Dad to Sarah's grandfather and back to Jack. He was waiting for his chance, too, but he was right in Jack's line of vision.

Sid saw a way.

I can get there. I can get behind him. If I'm careful.

He ducked low and hurried around the outside of the crowd. At the Post Office wall he ran through shadow, reached the edge of the steps, and crept to the top. Jack didn't seem to have noticed him. Then he inched across until he was directly above his dad's friend, looking down on him. Noiselessly, he took a step down, and then another.

His father's eyes never left Jack's, but Sid knew his dad had seen him. He was close enough now to see the sweat on his dad's forehead and the tremble in Jack's arm as he held the rifle.

Sid looked at Jack's wife. Her eyes were locked onto her husband. Her sons had seen him, though. They nodded, almost imperceptibly. He crept down another step. He was so close now, he could see the creases on the back of Jack's neck, and smell the gun oil.

"Jack?" said Dad. "Are you ready to come home now?" Dad's voice was gentle, conversational. He stepped a little closer. "Give me the rifle now, mate. Time to call it a day, eh?"

Jack wavered. He seemed on the point of surrendering his weapon, then Sid saw his whole body stiffen. He raised the rifle, his finger pressing against the trigger.

"NO!" Sid flung himself forward. He hit Jack's arm upwards with all his strength. A deafening roar made his head ring. The rifle spun in the air and smashed down on the stone steps. Pain shot through Sid's leg and he found himself lying next to Jack, watching a bright trickle of blood from beneath Jack's head run down onto the step below.

Chapter Twenty-Three

Ambulance

Jack! Sid stared at his dad's friend, sprawled on the steps. He wasn't moving. A pair of legs blocked his view, and Sid saw his father bending over his mate.

"Ambulance is here, Jack. They'll take care of you." Dad squatted down. "You'll be right."

Sid sat up, painfully. His head spun. Other men were arriving. Captain Findlay. Mr Thorndon. Jack's sons Peter and James were on the steps, gently rubbing their father's shoulders and holding his hand.

Captain Findlay picked up the gun and secured it. "Jack all right?" he asked.

"He's breathing," said Dad.

Two ambulance men pushed their way through the crowd. They laid a stretcher on the ground.

"What's his name?" one of them asked.

"Jack Riley," Dad answered.

Dad and Jack's sons made way for them. They squatted down on the steps next to Jack.

"All right, Mr Riley," said one of the men. "Just relax. We're here to help."

Jack groaned as they rolled him gently to examine his head.

"Nasty cut," said the other ambulance man. "Let's get you onto the stretcher, and we'll soon have it cleaned up."

"Are you all right, Sidney?" It was Mr Thorndon. "That was a brave thing you just did. Very brave."

Sid was unsure about what to say.

"Sit still," said Mr Thorndon. "I'll get the ambulance chaps to see you as well."

"I'm fine," said Sid.

"Just sit tight." Mr Thorndon's voice was firm.

Sid watched as they eased Jack onto the stretcher. He could see his face. There was a big cut over one eye.

Jack's eyes flicked open and found him. "Sidney," he said.

"Hello, Jack." Sid smiled. At least he could recognise people again.

One of the ambulance men put a hand on Jack's arm. "How are you feeling, Mr Riley?"

"Not too bad, son," said Jack. His face looked quite calm and relaxed, as if he had no idea what had just happened.

"Excuse me." It was Mr Thorndon. "When Jack is sorted out, there's another one here you should look at."

"Right you are, sir. We'll just get Mr Riley fixed up."

They were back in a few minutes.

"Is your name Sid?" asked one of the men.

"Yes," said Sid.

"He wants to talk to you, lad. Mr Riley does."

"Me?" Sid asked.

"Yes. He's very insistent. We told him he needs to rest, but he's getting agitated. So I said we'd fetch you."

Sid stood up. His head spun again, and he felt himself sway.

"I've got you, son." The ambulance man took his elbow and helped him down the steps. "I'm only giving you a couple of minutes with him, and don't excite him."

They led Sid to the open doors of the ambulance.

"Here he is, Mr Riley."

Sid looked in. Jack lay on a stretcher on one side and his wife was on a bench seat on the other. They were holding hands; their arms stretched out across the space between them.

"You can climb in, lad." The ambulance man nodded towards the vehicle. "Sit by Mrs Riley. I'll check your pulse while you talk to him. And then we'll have a look in your eyes."

Sid sat down, feeling the cool metal of the long bench seat under his hand as he steadied himself. The dim interior of the ambulance smelt like the inside of Mum's medicine cupboard. Jack's raspy breathing was loud in the small space. His chest rose and fell steadily under his thick flannel shirt.

The ambulance man took Sid's wrist. Sid felt two fingers pressing on his vein and kept still while the man concentrated, his eyes on his watch.

"Sidney." Jack's voice was wheezy. "I have a lot to thank you for."

"That's alright, Jack," said Sid awkwardly.

"You're a good boy. Your dad should be proud of you," said Jack.

The ambulance man released Sid's wrist. "Let's have a look in your eyes. Look at me."

Sid turned his head and tried not to blink as a bright light shone first into one eye and then into the other.

"What's your name, son?" asked the man.

"Sidney Everett."

"And do you know what day this is?"

"I should know," said Sid. "It's my birthday. The fourteenth of October. It's been a pretty unusual birthday so far."

"I think you'll do," said the ambulance man. "Just take it steady. Is someone from your family here?"

"Yes. My dad."

"That's good. You can have a few more words with Mr Riley now."

Sid turned back to Jack, whose bright eyes were still watching him.

"You're as brave as your father. A chip off the old block," said Jack.

"Don't flatter him, Jack. You'll make him big-headed." Dad appeared the doorway. He looked at Sid. "He's right. You're a brave boy. And a smart one."

"Arthur," said Jack. "Listen, before they take me wherever they're taking me, there's something I've got to say to you. About the boy. The racing. You have to listen to me, Arthur."

"I'm listening, Jack."

"It's his life. His dream, what he wants to be. It's not about you—you've had your go. Now it's his turn."

"I just wanted to save him from I went through," said Dad.

"They have to live their own lives," said Jack. "It'll be different for him."

Dad sighed. "I know." He glanced at Jack's wife, sitting small and still, her hand holding tight to Jack's. "I'm sure he'll be all right, Mrs Riley. He's in good hands."

"The family's hands are best," she said. "But I can see he needs help. For a bit."

She peered at Sid. "Are you all right, Sidney?"

"I'm fine, Mrs Riley."

Dad interrupted. "Sid, a policeman's arrived. I'm going to talk to him."

"Dad!" said Sid. "They wouldn't — they wouldn't put him in prison or anything?"

"I shouldn't think so. Hospital, I'd say. But I want to find out." He hurried away.

Sid turned back to Jack's wife. "I hope he'll be all right, Mrs Riley," he said.

"He will be, Sidney," she answered. She eyed him. "Sidney," she said, "there was something I wanted to tell your father. But you can tell him. He's going to get a letter."

Sid stared. "Is this another one of those matakite things?"

Her whole face crinkled up in a smile. "No. It's one of those 'who you know' things. My cousin works for the government in Wellington. She knows everything that's going on. The government is going to offer loans to returned servicemen. Like your dad, and my Jack. So they can buy some land."

"Truly?" asked Sid.

"Cross my heart," she said. "You tell your dad. It'll cheer him up."

"All right, everyone. We'll get this man into hospital." The ambulance men were kindly, but firm. "Out you hop, son."

Sid scrambled out.

One of the men took him by the elbow. "Steady now, lad. Is your dad still here?"

"Yes, somewhere," said Sid.

"Better find him, then," said the man.

The ambulance doors closed. Sid gazed around, looking for his dad.

"Here I am, son," Dad said.

"Arthur. Before you go." It was Mr Thorndon. "I've been talking with my father."

"How is he?" asked Dad.

Mr Thorndon grimaced. "Shocked, but he's all right. He'll be fine, in a bit." He cleared his throat. "He's very insistent that I talk to you about this boy here. Seems to think that bravery shouldn't go unrewarded."

Sid felt a wild leap of hope.

"And my daughter says the same. So, the offer is still there. For the apprenticeship."

Sid gasped.

Mr Thorndon turned and looked at him. "Your first job would be to look after Silver."

"Yes, sir!"

"And your second job would be to work extremely hard, doing whatever you're told to do."

"Yes, sir."

"And your third task is to turn yourself into that top jockey you want to be."

Chapter Twenty-Four

Just Desserts

Sid was mucking out the stables, enjoying the steady rhythm of the work and the pleasing smell of hay and horse manure in the dusty air. Sparrows chirped in the eaves overhead. The pile of old straw lay outside in the sunshine. He was almost finished, and thinking about going to find a wheelbarrow, when he heard Roger Dyson's voice.

He recognised that voice straight away. Loud and boastful. He moved to stand by the doorway, where he could watch without being seen.

Roger was standing by the track railing, his broad shoulders filling out a smart jacket. Sarah stood next to him, her blonde hair shining. She was wearing jodhpurs and a white cotton blouse. As Sid watched, Roger moved closer to her.

"Get away from her, you thug," Sid muttered. He clenched his fist on the handle of the pitchfork.

Sarah moved away. Sid was pleased to see it. He knew why Roger was here. He studied him carefully. His clothes were the best quality, Sid could tell that, even from a distance. His hair was smoothly combed to the side and gleaming with some kind of hair grease. He had a wide smile and his voice carried over to where Sid glowered in the shadows.

"Just dropped by to see if you want to go to the pictures with me. There's a new Bette Davis film. I know you're keen on Bette Davis."

"Oh, er, that's nice of you, Roger."

"Well, how about it? I never see you these days. And I'm off to Victoria, soon." He paused. "Pity you're not going there too."

"Hmmm." Sarah glanced over at the stable where Sid was working. He thought maybe she was hoping he would come to her rescue, but he suspected that this was one of those battles she had to fight alone. He stayed where he was.

"No thank you, Roger," she said. "I'd rather not. I'm a bit busy these days."

Roger followed her gaze. "Busy supervising the stable boy? I hope he's doing his job properly."

Sid felt a surge of anger.

That Dyson always has to say something snarky, to try and put someone else down. I've just about had enough.

But he didn't move; he wanted to hear Sarah's reply.

"If you mean Sid," said Sarah, "he's an apprentice jockey, not a stable boy." She drew herself up. "He's doing brilliantly, thank you. And he doesn't require any supervision. Dad says he's never had a better worker."

"That's surprising," said Roger. "He wasn't exactly brilliant at school. A bit slow, I would have said."

"Each to their own skills and talents, Roger," said Sarah. "He's doing what he loves. That's a lot more than most people ever do." She glared at him. "You'll be lucky if you end up being half as happy as he is."

"Landed on his feet, do you think?" Roger kicked a stone. "I wouldn't trust him with a horse of mine. Not many people would. The whole town knows about what he was doing, riding at night, on the beach. He almost killed your father's horse."

"Silver is fine, now." She raised her chin. "The whole town also knows about how brave he was, saving my grandad."

Roger was silent. Sid grinned to himself. He loosened his grip on the pitchfork, and it slipped out of his hand, clattering down onto the concrete slab, right in the doorway. He snatched it up and looked across the yard. Roger was coming over.

His bulk blocked out the sunlight. "Oh, it's the stable boy." He eyed the pitchfork in Sid's hand. "Hadn't you better get on with your work? Or did you stop to eavesdrop?"

Sid felt his cheeks burn. "I heard Sarah telling you she doesn't want to go to the pictures with you."

"She said, another time," said Roger.

Sarah was behind him. "No," she said. "Not another time."

Roger turned around.

Sarah wasn't smiling. "That wasn't what I said." She paused. "Good luck at university, Roger."

"Uh... Yes, good luck to you, too," said Roger.

"You might as well clear off now, Dyson." Sid's voice was steady. He remembered the pitchfork was still in his hand. As Roger turned again to look at him, he leaned it against the stable wall and squared his shoulders. "Good luck, Roger. All the best, at university."

Roger snorted and then walked away without looking back. Sid stepped out of the stable and stood next to Sarah, watching him go. He listened to the retreating footsteps fading away, slowly becoming aware of the birdsong, the sunshine, and the fragrance of Sarah's hair as she stood close beside him.

Chapter Twenty-Five

Like The Wind

Sid crouched low in the saddle, his heart racing, his horse's hooves pounding the turf as they flew around the Thornton's track.

Sarah was at the rail, stopwatch in hand. "Your best time ever," she called as he raced past.

As he slowed the horse, Sid leaned down to whisper in the dark ear, "Hear that, Silver? Best time ever!"

"Sidney!" Mr Thorndon called from the gate. "Your family's here."

Sid brought Silver to a standstill and looked over. His mother and father were approaching, followed by the twins and Ruby.

Dad spoke first. "Hello, son," he said.

"Hello." Sid glanced from one to the other. "This is it, then?"

"This is it," said Mum.

Sid dismounted, and Sarah took Silver's reins.

Mum gave him a hug. "Oh, Sidney, I can't believe it's happening."

"I'll miss you, Mum," said Sid. "I mean, I miss you already, even though you're only next door. But now..."

"Yes," she said, "it's a long way from here, Rangiora. But I've got family down there. It's like going home, for me."

Mr Thorndon shook Dad's hand. "All the best, Arthur."

"Thank you, Mr Thorndon. We're looking forward to it. Five acres and a house. All our own. Best thing to come out of the war."

"I'm very pleased for you." Mr Thorndon hesitated. "And what about your friend, Jack? How's he?"

"He's doing all right," said Dad. "He's not sure about taking the loan. His wife's family has land. He's been staying there since coming out of hospital."

"One step at a time, eh?" said Mr Thorndon.

"Yes," said Dad. "One step at a time."

Mr Thorndon turned to Mum. "Well, Mrs Everett. I wish you and your family all the very best."

"Thank you, Mr Thorndon. I think it's going to work out well for us. Beryl's coming too. She's going to train to be a teacher in Christchurch. And Ruby will go to the Sumner School for deaf children."

"And the twins?"

"Oh, they can't wait," said Mum. "And I know they'll love it down there."

Sid looked at his brothers. A new life. One he wouldn't share. It was a strange feeling.

"Sidney?" It was Dad. "Sid, I'm very proud of you."

Sid met his eyes, feeling a new current of warmth and understanding pass between them. "Thanks, Dad," he said.

"And something else," said Dad.

"Yes, Dad?"

"I want you to know that every time you win a race, I'm going to cut out the newspaper article about you, and I'm going to pin it up on the wall."

Sid laughed. "Seriously?"

"Yes," said Dad. "When you come to visit, you can see them all."

"I'll come and visit. Definitely," said Sid.

Dad nodded. He reached up a hand and stroked Silver's neck. "I watched you just now. You and Silver. You were going like the wind."

Sid smiled. "Like the wind," he said.

Also By J L Williams

Like The Wind is the dramatic sequel to Holding The Horse. Sid Everett is about to ride in the race of his dreams when his attempts to aid a vagrant World War II veteran end in disaster. Can he redeem his good name before the NZ Cup race begins, or has his determination to do the right thing destroyed his dream of glory forever?
A fast paced and heart-warming story.

Acknowledgments

My heartfelt thanks to all those who encouraged me and believed in Sid's story. I would especially like to acknowledge Janice Marriott, my mentor, for choosing my manuscript as the winner of the inaugural Janice Marriott Mentoring Award. Without Janice, the manuscript would most likely have never been finished. Also Storylines New Zealand, for shortlisting my manuscript for the Tom Fitzgibbon Award. Lisette de Jong, my lovely editor. Penelope Foote, my first reader, for all of her knowledge of horses and horse behaviour. My husband Andrew for his patience. My sister Fran, who always believed in me, and my mother, who always said "You could write a book about that."

About The Author

J L Williams lives in the north of New Zealand on ten acres of land with her husband, her dog, a horse, a cat, several sheep and chickens and lots of fruit trees.

She loves children's books and writing and holidays by the sea.

Website: www.jlwilliamsauthor.com